HOPE

Project Go Green

H♥PE
Project Go Green

By Alyssa Milano
with Debbie Rigaud

ILLUSTRATED BY ERIC S. KEYES

Scholastic Inc.

Library of Congress Cataloging-in-Publication Data available

ISBN 978-1-338-32943-8

1 2021

Printed in the U.S.A.   23

First printing 2021

Book design by Katie Fitch

This book is dedicated to all the young people who are fighting every day to make the world a better place. You give me hope.

—A. M.

For Bernard. And with
special thanks to Grace Gordon!

—D. R.

To Ollie, his friends and all of the kids who have enjoyed following Hope on her journey.

—E. K.

HOPE

Project Go Green

Chapter I

"This way, explorers!" bellows the animated camp counselor in the yellow Camp Go Green T-shirt. Her waist-length braids swing back and forth as she climbs up a knobby mound of dirt to get a better view of our group.

I can't believe we're in the great outdoors surrounded by a real forest. Our entire grade, plus the JFK Middle School science club, just arrived here in a caravan of buses. The long ride went by faster than I expected. As soon as we stepped off the bus, we were assigned different Camp Go Green counselors and separated into groups.

My best friend, Sam, turns to me, her wide eyes

flashing with alarm. "Do you think there are any bears in this forest?" she asks.

"We've waited so long for this class trip," I say sadly. "It would be a huge bummer if we all got eaten."

Sam's mouth drops open like she's on her first roller-coaster ride, and I throw my arm around her shoulders and giggle.

Once our camp counselor makes it to the top of the dirt mound, head and shoulders above the crowd, she waves her arms and announces, "Welcome to Camp Go Green! I'm Ms. Gordon, your guide for this two-day stay. It's a pleasure hosting JFK Middle School. And it's an honor being your camp counselor."

"Do you think ours is one of the hiking groups or one of the tour groups?" Sam whispers to me.

I glance at the groups already being led to a giant log cabin, on their way to view the camp's indoor facilities. It wouldn't bother me if we didn't follow. I'm just so excited I'm in the same group as Sam and my good friends Camila, Grace, and Chloe. Most of the guys from the science club are also in the group—including my rude classmate Connor and his sidekick, Shep. But having Henry Chen here, too, makes up for it.

"She doesn't look like the indoor-tour type," I answer Sam, taking in Ms. Gordon's hike-ready outfit and the sizable backpack strapped to her shoulders.

A bird trills somewhere above us, and Ms. Gordon smiles. "You hear that warm welcome, explorers?" she says, a playful glint in her eyes. "A little birdie told me you'll make the most of this trip. Just consider this your home for the next two days."

"Uh, does that mean we'll be camping in the woods?" asks Connor, his voice traveling over our heads.

"Well, no, you'll be sleeping indoors," replies Ms. Gordon, and a few people around me—including Sam and Camila—give loud sighs of relief. Ms. Gordon holds up a finger. "But with its amazing views and all-natural construction, the Cabin is the next closest thing to outdoor living. I'll give you a tour of our facilities soon. For now, you've got more bird concerts to enjoy, majestic trees to walk among, and trails to blaze!"

"Plus, bears to run from?" Sam whispers to me.

Chloe and Grace, who are standing in front of us, turn around and giggle with Sam.

"Are you ready for a hike?" Ms. Gordon shouts cheerfully.

Everyone nods or mumbles their replies, except me. I'm pumped. I can't wait to hear and see more.

"Yes!" I shout back, not expecting to be the only one.

Thankfully, Sam and Camila echo my shout right away to cover me.

"Good looking out, guys," I mutter to them, and they giggle before shooting me matching thumbs-ups.

Ms. Gordon leads the way, and as we break through the tree line, suddenly a dense forest surrounds us on all sides. In here, the crunching sounds of leaves and twigs under our feet seem to be amplified. Even the bird calls echo!

"Aah, they're starting the concert with my

favorite song," jokes Ms. Gordon. Or is she not joking? I can't help but smile.

Ms. Gordon continues bellowing as we follow her deeper into the woods. "Keep an eye out for flying squirrels . . . ," she says.

As I listen closely, I begin to outpace Sam and Camila and walk past Chloe and Grace.

I get so absorbed in Ms. Gordon's nature facts that—*whoops!* My toe hooks under a knobby tree root and . . . I trip.

And fall.

Right into a mud puddle!

I'm totally mortified. I don't even make an effort to get up. Maybe, just maybe, it's safer to stay where I am, on my hands and knees.

Snickering breaks out, and I can easily identify the loudest chuckle as Connor's. I wonder how long I'll have to pretend to be a statue before the group loses interest and just walks on by.

"Woman down, Ms. Gordon," someone alerts our camp counselor.

She whips around and spies me.

Great. Everyone's still here.

At that moment, I feel a gentle tug on my arm, encouraging me to stand. I look up at the owner of the helping hand, and my eyes meet Henry's.

"Are you okay?" he asks, raising me to my feet.

I nod bashfully. "I'm fine," I tell him.

My cheeks grow hot, and I'm not entirely sure if it's because I'm embarrassed I fell in front of so many witnesses, or if it's for another reason. A Henry-shaped reason.

"You're all right," says Ms. Gordon, who's also now at my side. "It's a good thing the earth caught ya!"

A few kids laugh at Ms. Gordon's joke, their eyes all still on me.

"Hope, are you hurt?" asks a worried Sam, who has just rushed over, with Camila, Grace, and Chloe right behind her.

"No." I fake a chuckle. "I'm fine—not hurt at all. No big deal. Can we just keep the tour going?"

"Looks like she needs to go to the Cabin to clean off whatever *that* is," says Connor, walking over and pointing to my leg.

I look down and see a glob of mud slowly sliding down from one knee onto my calf. Without thinking, I reach down and wipe it off, but now my hand is super muddy.

Connor takes an exaggerated step backward like he's afraid of dirt. "Don't wipe that on me."

"Anyone have a tissue?" I ask, cringing. We just got here, and already I'm a mess. The only person carrying anything is Ms. Gordon. The rest of us were instructed to leave our things on the luggage carts lined up by the buses. But Ms. Gordon doesn't reach into her backpack, and now more people are joining in with Connor's immature snickering.

"No scrapes," Ms. Gordon says, finishing her close inspection of me. "It's only a little mud— nature's spa treatment."

"Hope, you are so lucky we couldn't bring our phones," Connor teases, miming like he's snapping a picture of my muddy hand and knees.

Ugh, make it stop.

Suddenly, Henry is moving. He reaches down and scoops up a handful of mud and scrapes it across his own calf.

"You're right, Ms. Gordon," he says, though he's looking—and smiling—right at me. "It's only mud."

I almost cover my mouth with my soiled hand but stop myself in the nick of time, my palm hovering

inches from my lips. That's when we both bust out laughing at my near miss. We keep laughing at the state of our muddy legs, and suddenly I feel all the cringe just melt away.

"Thank you, Henry," I say, still smiling.

Ms. Gordon interrupts the moment to hand me a soft and fuzzy leaf. "Try this," she says with a wink. "There are natural and biodegradable tissues all around us."

I smile and wipe my hands with the leaf. It works pretty well. The show over now, Ms. Gordon gets us all moving again. Sam, Grace, Chloe, and Camila are at my side as we follow.

Ms. Gordon heads down a rocky hill lined with thinner trees. Sam and I let go of each other's arms so that we can keep our balance trekking downhill. My hiking boots loosen a few pebbles and they tumble farther down, but I stay upright this time.

Though her back is facing us, I can tell Ms. Gordon is super excited because her head is bobbing and she's pointing this way and that as she talks. "Like with any new friend you meet, it's good to share your backstories," I hear Ms. Gordon say. "So, let me tell you about your pal the Camp Go Green

forest. Sure, today she's a preserved area. But not
too long ago, this forest was going to be razed and
turned into a highway off-ramp."

Sam puts her hand to her heart in surprise.
A few others gasp. My friends and I edge toward
the front of the group as we try to get closer to
Ms. Gordon. I don't want to miss a word of what she's
saying.

Ms. Gordon nods and turns her profile to us as
she throws her voice over her shoulder. "Yup, imagine what that would be like. The air wouldn't be
this clean, for one. Can anyone think of any other
changes losing this forest would cause?"

"The animals would lose their habitat," says
Henry.

"People wouldn't get to enjoy this amazing view," answers Chloe, looking around in awe.

"Yeah, this place is unbelievable," another class-mate exclaims.

"How did you save the forest?" I call out.

"Oh, with lots of effort," says Ms. Gordon. "It took the entire community pitching in, collecting peti-tion signatures all over the county, and convincing the landowners not to sell." Ms. Gordon claps once, but thunderously. "Whoo! It was a huge victory."

She finally stops at a small clearing and waits for everyone to catch up. From there, we can hear and see flowing water a little farther ahead. It looks like a narrow river or creek. The cooler rush of air from the water feels refreshing.

Once every last one of us is accounted for, Ms. Gordon waits for the murmuring and chuckles to fade away. Her stillness is all the hint we need. Little by little, our chatter dies down until the only sound left is the trickling of water over smooth stones.

"This river is perfect for skipping rocks, but that's not why we're visiting this site today," Ms. Gordon begins. She slips her huge backpack off her narrow shoulders and places it on a boulder. She opens the flap and pulls out mini wooden plaques. Even though they look small and lightweight, it's a wonder Ms. Gordon fit them all in her bag. There are enough plaques for each one of us in the group. "The wonderful folks in our gift shop used their handy laser printing machine to create these personalized messages."

Ms. Gordon calls out our first names, one by one, and we walk over to collect our plaque. I examine mine when it's finally in my hands, and it begins to make sense why the camp needed our email addresses before we got here.

The message reads: *We are middle school students conducting an experiment. Please email me with the location you found this. Thank you!*

"By now you've all received a plaque and read its message," says Ms. Gordon, smirking at us with a raised eyebrow. "Anyone want to guess what we're about to do with them?"

Grace raises her hand, and Ms. Gordon points to her.

"Toss them in the stream and see how far they go?" asks Grace.

"Exactly that! And not to worry—these plaques are biodegradable, so if no one finds them, they will dissolve in a reasonably short time," explains Ms. Gordon.

We all check the wood-like material again, and this time I realize it gives when I pinch it. Pretty cool.

Ms. Gordon continues. "But until then—or until it's found—this plaque will continue following where the stream leads, to bigger rivers, to lakes or reservoirs, and ultimately to the ocean. It's a reminder of how our ecosystem is all interconnected. So, that means what we do in one natural setting can impact another—no matter how far away."

We follow Ms. Gordon out of the clearing and closer to the stream's edge.

"After dropping in your plaque, you're welcome to dip your toes in the water," says Ms. Gordon. "Or find what we at Camp Go Green call your sit spot. A sit spot is a peaceful place where you can sit quietly and just chill with nature. Think, observe, be still."

A few kids remove their socks and shoes and

wade into the water to release their plaque. Others walk away from the group and find a less crowded area to drop it in. I hold on to my plaque a little longer, feeling the grooves of the etched message, hoping it finds someone who is excited to email me news of its final destination.

A few minutes later, I stand at the edge of the water and watch the current carry my plaque away. I wonder about the likelihood that it'll be found by a person instead of some beaver that has no idea what the Internet is.

Either way, this is such a cool start to our field trip. I can't wait to see what Ms. Gordon has in store next.

Chapter 2

After our hike, Ms. Gordon takes us back to see Camp Go Green's facilities. Everyone calls the big building at the center of camp the Cabin, but it's way bigger than you'd expect a building like that to be.

Our indoor tour is a lot less magical than the outdoor one, but very cool just the same.

"This is a green facility, meaning we built this entire complex with the environment in mind," says Ms. Gordon as she leads us through the lobby area, under its sky-high ceilings. "A lot of the building materials are recycled, we use solar energy for power, and we catch rainwater in a belowground tank. There's a working farm, and we even compost a lot of our waste."

The more Ms. Gordon talks about all the camp does for the environment, the closer I pay attention. It's such a selfless, thoughtful way to think.

"What's composting?" someone asks.

Ms. Gordon stops next to a floor-to-ceiling window, and as we listen to her answer, we get an amazing view of the river.

"I'm glad you asked that," she says. "One thing we're always trying to get better at here is reducing

waste. That means minimizing the stuff we have to throw in the trash. Just like in your homes, whatever we trash gets picked up by the sanitation truck, which then delivers it to a landfill. Most of the trash in landfills never goes away. Composting allows us to collect our organic trash in a different way. Come, let me show you."

Ms. Gordon walks so much faster indoors than she did outside. We speed-walk to a big but cozy cafeteria that looks a little smaller than the one at our school.

Camila turns to us and says, "I wonder what they're making for lunch."

"Whatever it is, it smells yummy," answers Sam.

"Here in our canteen, we don't have any disposable plates, utensils, or napkins," notes Ms. Gordon.

Our friendly camp counselor waves to everyone working in the kitchen as we walk by, and they wave back. Out a back door near the kitchen is a giant compost bin. It's about the size of a minivan but short enough to peer into if we stand on our tiptoes. Ms. Gordon lifts the lid to show us the mix of what looks like soil and leaves inside.

"We add food scraps from the cafeteria and other biodegradable items to this compost pile, and it turns into fertilizer we can use in our garden. It's great for the soil, and it helps us use less water, too," explains Ms. Gordon.

"It doesn't smell as bad as I thought it would," says Grace, releasing her pinch grip on her nose.

"That's because our lunch smells so good, I can't pick up any other scent," Chloe responds.

"Ooh, that reminds me," says Ms. Gordon, holding up a finger in a way we've already become used to. "You guys are responsible for dinner tonight."

Everyone reacts at once. There's a chorus of:

"Huh?"

"We are?"

"Seriously?"

"You heard right," says Ms. Gordon, a sly grin on her face. "Tonight for dinner, you're all pitching in to feed your fellow classmates. I volunteered our group for that task. Are you up for the challenge?"

"If we say no, does that mean we'll get out of it?" Shep asks hopefully.

"Not a chance." Ms. Gordon smiles back broadly. "But for now, how about you all go get settled into your rooms before lunch? After you've eaten, I'll meet you in the cafeteria and we'll get started on dinner prep."

Ms. Gordon gets zero complaints about her suggestion that we check out our rooms and eat.

My friends and I all look at one another and squeal. Ever since we found out the five of us could room together, we've been super excited.

A breathless climb to the third floor later, we're in our room, reuniting with our luggage and phones, taking quick selfies, and choosing our preferred beds—I'll bunk with Sam, Grace will bunk with Chloe, and Camila gets the single bed.

We get to lunch early enough to grab our food and claim a table next to a giant window.

"That long ride plus the hike really worked up my appetite," says Grace, looking down at our trays of chicken fajitas.

Camila's mouth is already full. "Everything tastes so good," she says. A few diced tomatoes spill out of her salsa as she takes another bite.

"The views are pretty, plus the food is amazing?" I say, shaking my head in disbelief.

"Now we know why Ms. Gordon is so cheerful all the time," Sam laughs.

"I think she's cheerful because she loves what she does, and she's good at it," I say. "She gets people to really care about the planet."

My friends nod, either because they agree with what I said or they're loving how tasty lunch is. I can't tell which.

As I chomp down my fajita in record time, I think about how Ms. Gordon is like my favorite comic book hero. Galaxy Girl is all about protecting the universe, and Ms. Gordon is all about protecting the earth.

Once we're done eating, we have no utensils, straws, napkins, or wrappers to toss in the trash. Our cutlery and dishes are made from reusable bamboo, so we leave them on a conveyer belt to the kitchens after scraping our leftovers into a compost bin. The Cabin really practices what they preach about reducing waste.

Ms. Gordon arrives just as a few of us are gathering at a large cafeteria table, chatting. She listens for a few minutes, as if curious about our opinions.

"This canteen is so different than our cafeteria at school," says one girl.

"I still can't believe I didn't have *any* trash to throw away," I reply.

A few kids nod and share their own thoughts. Once the rest of the group finishes their lunch and heads over to our group table, Ms. Gordon asks, "Is everyone here?"

We all nod, and Ms. Gordon escorts our group out of the canteen. We follow her into the kitchen, and the group comes to a stop, some kids finding corners to stand in and walls to lean on.

"Why'd everyone stop here?" Ms. Gordon asks us. "We're just passing through the kitchen. Come with me."

My friends and I look at one another with a *Huh?* look on our faces.

We all follow Ms. Gordon as she walks outside, past the compost, and through a gate that leads to a wide-open field with the healthiest, most thriving garden I've ever seen.

"This is nice," I sigh.

"I'm glad you think so, Hope." Ms. Gordon smiles at me. I smile back, admiring all the cool ways she is working on her Save the Planet mission. "Everyone, this is Camp Go Green's garden," she announces to the group. "We grow almost everything that our camp cook needs to create your delicious meals. So the veggies and herbs you harvest this afternoon will help create tonight's dinner."

A few sighs of relief break out.

"So that means we won't have to cook it?"

Ms. Gordon laughs and shakes her head, and we all cheer.

We walk through a large field with neat rows of vegetation poking out from the dark soil. Everything is so carefully arranged. It's unlike any garden I've ever seen. My parents take good care of our houseplants, but I wouldn't say they exactly have green thumbs.

Ms. Gordon gives us a tour of the garden, explaining how it's all set up—herbs to one side, root veggies in another corner, and veggies on vines opposite there. "See what a giving friend the earth is?"

Everyone is buzzing like the garden's bees, excitedly pointing out the veggies they recognize. Of course, Camila is excited to see a few herbs she uses in her family bakery, like peppermint.

"Okay, okay," Ms. Gordon chuckles, tickled by our reaction. "How about you all grab a basket and a pair of garden gloves and get started. Our talented gardeners and I will be walking around, helping you identify which veggies are ready for harvest."

Walking through the garden feels like going to the produce department in a supermarket, except there are no clear plastic bags you can never open on the first try, or boring music on the loudspeakers. I pull lettuce with the help of a gardener who points out the ideal color, size, and crispness of the leafy greens. I also grab a few string beans, which are a lot easier to identify.

"What did you get?" I ask Grace.

"A few herbs, which will be great for seasoning the food. And a few bell peppers."

"You guys, if I pull the green tomatoes off the vine, someone can make fried green tomatoes!" says Camila.

"What a harvest!" shouts Ms. Gordon, calling us over with our baskets. "Everything looks beautiful."

We load our baskets onto waiting carts, and a few kitchen aides dressed all in white thank us before they wheel everything away.

When we leave the garden, I feel like my thumbs would literally be green if I looked at them closely enough.

"That was a lot more fun than I thought it would be," says Sam.

"I know," I admit. "It was really cool pulling veggies out of the ground that will actually feed people!"

"It's a good feeling," agrees Camila.

"Yup," I say with a smile. "It feels good helping the planet."

And I can't wait to help out more.

☺❀♆

Later that day, we feast on a dinner of vegetable casserole and a fresh salad in the cafeteria. Our dessert is roasted s'mores at the firepit deeper in the forest.

We watch the sun go down and have our fill of toasted marshmallows and campfire stories. When we think the night is over, Ms. Gordon asks, "Who wants to go on a night hike?" Of course the answer is *everyone*.

Walking into a dark forest takes some bravery. It's not as scary as I'd imagined it to be. But that doesn't seem to be the case for Sam, who keeps squeezing my arm tighter.

"You okay?" I ask my bestie.

"Just fine," she says. "I'm not thinking of bear attacks at all."

"I'm pretty sure we need to worry more about mosquitoes attacking than bears," I say. Even though I sprayed bug spray everywhere and I'm wearing tall hiking boots, I still don't trust the bugs.

"What we need right now are some bats to come out," says Grace.

"What?" Sam looks horrified.

"To eat the bugs," Grace explains.

We all crack up at Sam's expression.

After a while, Sam's grip loosens on my arm, and we just enjoy the stroll.

"The next time you're at the forest or even a park, enjoy the greenery and make it your true-blue friend," Ms. Gordon says as she leads the way. "If we can show love and respect for ourselves, each other, and even our pets, what's stopping us from doing the same for our planet?"

I listen to Ms. Gordon's voice. What she's saying makes so much sense. And then, before I know it, we're deeper inside the forest than I ever imagined I'd go—especially at night.

I look up and all around, pointing my flashlight in every direction until Ms. Gordon reaches a large tree and asks us to turn off all the lights.

"If we give our eyes time to adjust, we may see the bioluminescent foxfire mushroom patch that's somewhere around here."

"Whoa," someone says as we pick up a soft green glow. It looks sort of like the color of fireflies, except this doesn't blink.

It's so awesome. And I still can't believe it's always been here for us.

When we get back to our room, we're too pooped to stay up and chat. The calming forest sounds lull us all quickly to sleep.

☺♻🌳

Day two at Camp Go Green is just as cool. Sam, Camila, Grace, Chloe, and I run through as many of the offered activities as we can—a woodworking

class in the morning, spending an artsy afternoon painting a beautiful forest scene, and taking a fun dip in the swimming hole later in the day.

It's true time flies when you're having fun, because after an early dinner, we're all in the parking lot saying goodbye to our camp counselors.

"Thank you, Ms. Gordon," I say as my classmates file into our waiting buses. "This trip was so amazing."

Ms. Gordon raises a finger. "Nature has the power to amaze. All we need to do is care for it and pay closer attention so we don't harm it," she says.

"Well, I'm paying attention now," I say. "And I want to help in any way I can."

Chapter 3

"**S**ounds like it was a fantastic class trip," my dad says, his voice rising above all the murmuring in this busy restaurant.

I nod at him with a big grin on my face. "It was."

My mom, my dad, my sister, Marie, and I are all seated in a sunlit booth. Most of the dinner plates still crowding our tabletop are nearly empty—except mine.

"Did you like your dinner?" Mom asks me, eyeing my piled-on pasta and veggies. "You hardly ate."

I look down at my plate and grimace. "I guess I've been so excited, I forgot to eat."

"More like you've been so *chatty*, you forgot to

eat," cracks Marie. She reaches her fork over and nabs a few noodles before I can swat her away.

"Please, feel free to help yourself," I say, my voice dipped in syrupy sarcasm.

Marie grimaces mid-chew. "Ew, no thanks. Your food's gotten cold."

"That's okay," my dad says to us while gesturing to our server. "We'll take this and our desserts to go."

I know that overwhelmed look on Dad's face. He's thinking about all the work he has to do. Normally my dad is pretty easygoing, but since we're only about a month from NASA's upcoming rocket launch, Dad—like every other scientist he works with—has a lot going on.

It's the biggest, most important event this year for Dad and his team (and also for me, as a future astrophysicist). But it's also a super-stressful time for Dad, since the whole city—and country—are eagerly awaiting the launch.

Mom gives me a smile, even as her eyes dart around the restaurant in search of our server. My mom is busy with work, too. She's brainstorming her gallery's major public arts project. It happens once a year, and it's a huge deal for the whole county.

"To-go containers for the awesome family in booth nine," announces the bubbly server as she sets the stack of empty cartons on our table.

My mom smiles and thanks the server before she zips away. "Girls, hurry and pack up your food so we can head home."

I freeze and look at the white containers like they're crawling with spiders, because . . . polystyrene. According to Camp Go Green's website (which I scrolled through on my phone during our bus ride home), the ridged plastic foam material (that's kind of like Styrofoam) is not biodegradable. I mean, goodness—it sticks around in landfills and oceans for like a million years.

"What's the matter, baby?" Mom asks.

I shake my head. "Uh—I don't need to bring my leftovers home."

"But then all that food is going to go to waste," Mom replies.

Waste. Ugh. I don't want to be wasteful, either. Do I? As soon as the question floats into my mind, I think of something Ms. Gordon said at camp. *This friendship with the environment doesn't end here. Keep looking out for the earth, just like any pal would.* I know what to do. Just as Marie is about to drop her triple-layer chocolate mousse cake into a container, I yank the take-out box away from her.

Her eyes are like daggers. "Hey!"

"I'll be right back," I tell my family as I step out of our booth.

Cradling the stack of containers, I flag down our friendly server. She looks surprised, but she greets me with a cheerful "How can I help you?"

"Hi, Tatiana?" I start, double-checking her name tag to make sure I remembered her name correctly. "I was wondering, do you have any different containers—maybe cardboard? It's just that these are bad for the environment. I know a lot of restaurants no longer use them, so I didn't expect—"

"I know what you mean," says Tatiana. "I kept bringing it up with my manager—over and over again—and she finally agreed to make the switch." She pretends to wipe sweat from her brow in relief. "These containers happen to be the last batch of their kind, but I can grab you a few new ones."

"Thanks!" I tell her when she returns, handing me the biodegradable containers. I return her warm smile with one of my own.

"And thank you," I say.

She nods in understanding. "Hey, if we don't look out for the environment, who will?"

"Wow, this trip really made an impression on you," says Mom, beaming with pride when I return with the new containers.

I nod and realize that I feel good for speaking up for the earth. "It did."

⊕♻♆

When my family and I get home, our rescue pups, Cosmo and Rocket, are there to greet us with sloppy kisses and *paw-fect* cuddles. I barely step into the kitchen before they're brushing against my legs and keeping pace with my every step. That's their catlike way of asking me to take them out for a stroll.

"Okay, you two." I grin down at them. "Let's hit the streets."

Dad will appreciate that I'm taking the dogs out. He's the one who usually has evening-walk honors. Although I often go with him, it's nice having this time alone with the dogs after a couple of days away. It's also nice knowing I'm taking one thing off Dad's to-do list for tonight.

When I got back from camp last night, I could tell Cosmo and Rocket had missed me. Even now, they keep turning around to look at me, as if checking to make sure I'm still here. I chuckle and give them a treat.

"What, do you two greedy goobers think your leashes are holding themselves? I'm no magician."

I'm nearly home after our circle around the block when I notice a few bins lining the sidewalk. It's both trash day and recycling pickup tomorrow, but it's windy tonight. Someone's loose trash is already swirling in the breeze. I pick up the litter and toss it into the nearest bin. When I reach our home, I can't believe how piled high our bins are. Our open lids look like the mouth of someone laughing with their mouth full. We have more trash than the Jeongs, who have twice as many people in their family, if you count their visiting grandparents. Through the stretched white garbage bag, I spot take-out containers, plastic coffee cups, and even clothes. All

these things could've been donated or recycled.

The memory of what Ms. Gordon said about Camp Go Green swirls in my mind: *We work hard at reducing waste.*

Meanwhile, it looks like my family hardly works at reducing waste. Our carbon footprint will be T. rex–size if I don't step in—fast. I know I was only at Camp Go Green for two days, but I think I know enough of the basics of environmentalism and conservation to launch a Go Green challenge at home. I realize Dad's busy with his rocket launch, and Mom and Marie are busy, too, but saving the planet is critical, and it can't wait.

Chapter 4

The next morning, I wake up eager to bring the camp's lessons home. But the question is, how?

Camp Go Green didn't give out leaflets or flyers, because . . . paper waste. So it's a good thing I discovered their amazing website during the long bus ride. I log back in to start coming up with my at-home action plan.

A sigh escapes from Rocket even though she's still half asleep. She and Cosmo are sprawled on my bedroom floor, inches away from where I sit at my desk.

"Now you sound like Marie." I reach down and scratch between Rocket's ears. "Is all my talk about Camp Go Green not exciting to you?"

With the way these two are lazing around, you'd think they worked the night shift.

I browse through a few of Camp Go Green's web pages. On one, I find a small section with bios and career highlights for Ms. Gordon and the other Camp Go Green counselors.

"A real park ranger? So cool!" I say to myself, since Cosmo and Rocket clearly aren't listening. I glance down to confirm they're sound asleep and then continue reading about how Ms. Gordon used to be a park ranger  in the Smoky Mountains. I feel even luckier that we got to meet her and have her as our counselor.

When I finally get to the page I've been searching for, I grab my dry-erase board and scribble a few ideas down. There's so much good stuff here. I find all sorts of cool tips about reducing waste in households. It looks like a lot of the handy charts and simple to-do lists were written by Ms. Gordon herself.

Once I have a good starting point, it's time to take some notes about my observations, like any good scientist would.

The minute I step out of my room, Marie walks by with an iced-coffee cup in her hand.

"Hey, how's Diya?" I ask her about her best friend.

"Oh, she's fine. I just met up with her at the coffee shop, and we banged out a little bit of our group project. It's worth half our grade, and there's so much more to do."

"Cool that you started," I say, walking to the kitchen while jotting down some notes: *need reusable thermoses.*

Once I'm in the kitchen, I look in the fridge and count four different take-out containers. Because everyone's been so busy, we've been ordering in dinner more than ever, and there's the evidence. I take to my dry-erase board and scribble: *reusable containers.*

Next, I look in some of the counter drawers and come across one that's full of plastic bags from the supermarket. I stop and make another note: *reusable shopping bags.*

I keep up my scientific observations all day, and

the list grows. On a spare poster board, I copy a really cool waste-tracker chart from the camp's website. By dinnertime, I have a better understanding of my family's patterns, so I text the family thread.

Request for a family meeting? I type. *I only need about ten minutes.*

After about five minutes, I hear from both my parents.

Sure, I could use a quick break, responds Dad.

Meet you on the family room couch in fifteen, answers my mom.

Another five minutes pass and still no word from Marie. I march to my door, swing it open, and shout into the hallway.

"Marie?"

Her muffled shriek sounds her reply. "All right! I'll be there!"

Smiling to myself, I double-check the chart I made and review the notes on my dry-erase board. Then it's time to meet Mom, Dad, and Marie.

We haven't had our usual family movie night in a while, so it's nice to meet up like this—if only for a chat.

"I know you're all super busy, so I'll make this quick," I say, standing before my parents, who are waiting patiently on the couch.

My dad looks more relaxed than he did last night at the restaurant. He's wearing his reading glasses on his head and keeps his legs stretched and crossed at the ankle, with one arm around the back of the couch. Mom is munching on a chewy snack bar that smells like blueberries, and I stop short of asking her if there are any more.

"As soon as Marie gets here, I'll start."

I cup my hands around my mouth. "Marie!" I shout.

She shuffles down the hall into the living room, her eyes glued to her cell screen. "I'm coming! But make this quick. We're all super busy."

I look at my parents for a beat before the three of us shake our heads and start cracking up.

Marie looks confused. "Did I miss something?"

"Yes, exactly that," teases Mom, who playfully tugs at Marie's arm. "Now come take a seat so Hope can get started."

"Thank you." I take a deep breath. My family has always had my back and been good sports about helping me reach the goals I set for myself, my school, or my community. I know they don't have a lot of time right now, but I'm hoping they will be cool with me putting something else on their plates. I think it's worth bringing up, especially because this is something that takes practice and will ultimately help us all.

Dad gives me an encouraging smile, but I catch him checking his phone for the time.

"As you know, I learned a lot at Camp Go Green. My two days there have caused me to see things in a different light, like the way we live as a family," I say. "For a family of four, we have entirely too much waste. We need to cut down, and I know just how we can do that."

I reach for the poster board leaning on the recliner behind me, and turn it to face everyone.

"This is a trash census. It's a chart you can fill out with all the items you toss out each day." My parents'

eyes are thoughtfully scanning the poster's graphics and charts. But Marie lets out a dramatic sigh.

"Come on, are you for real?" she asks. "With all that's going on, how do you expect us to be that detailed about everything?"

I pause and think about how preoccupied my parents have been lately. Maybe if I get things started on my own and cover their duties for a while, they'll all see why this is important—and that it's not a huge deal to make a few small changes. Then, hopefully, they'll be inspired to pick up their slack and keep it going.

"You're right," I answer Marie with a little reverse psychology. I mentally high-five myself when my answer takes everyone by surprise. Marie especially. She looks like she can't enjoy the victory of me publicly admitting she's right, because she's so thrown off by it.

"And that's why I'll handle everything. I've formed a Go Green team with a volunteer who will help me keep track of your waste," I say, making this up as I go along. "We'd only need to monitor one or two random days. Each of you will toss any trash you make that day into your own designated bag. Then my volunteer and I will collect those bags and report our findings back to you."

"Yuck," hollers Marie. "Digging into other people's trash is *not* a job I would sign up for. Who is this volunteer who doesn't mind literally getting their hands dirty?"

"Sam," I say, clearing my throat. What I don't add is "I hope." You see, I haven't exactly asked Sam yet, but that's what best friends are for—right?

"Are you sure about this, Hope?" Mom asks. "It sounds like it's a lot for you take on, and a lot to ask of a friend."

"I can handle looking through the trash on my own, if it comes to it. And she can still help with charting and weighing the bags."

To get everyone away from the trash-digging topic, I grab the dry-erase board leaning against the coffee table and move on with my presentation. I mention the goal of tackling the three Rs—reduce, reuse, recycle. Next I briefly explain the categories I'll be sorting—like packaging, food waste, and paper waste—over the twenty-four-hour periods.

"This has all the makings of a solid scientific study," Dad says, impressed. "Measuring individual waste as well as household waste should bring up some interesting results."

Knowing my dad feels proud makes my smile stretch clear across my face.

"I gotta admit, I'm curious how we'll do," says Marie as she stands up from the couch and pulls her phone out of her back pocket.

Taking a cue from Marie, Mom and Dad both stand and stretch as if they've been seated a long time.

"Well, I want to thank you guys in advance for cooperating," I say before they file out of the family room. "I hope to make this as painless as possible for everyone. Starting tomorrow you'll find trash bins with your initials on them set up in the garage. Just toss your trash bags in your bin, and I'll handle the rest."

The first thing I do when I get back to my room is text Sam an SOS. Fingers crossed, she'll say yes.

Chapter 5

On Monday, the first day back at school after the class trip, my classmates had all been swapping funny stories and reminiscing about being in the forest and bonding with camp counselors. But by Friday, everyone at our science club meeting has pretty much stopped gushing about Camp Go Green. Well, everyone except me.

"Hey, do you guys ever wonder how far our river messages went?" I ask Camila and Grace as we grab a seat in the lab's large workstation to wait for Mr. Gillespie to start our meeting. We could probably kick off the meeting ourselves, but as our faculty adviser, Mr. G. usually makes a few announcements before we get started.

Mr. Gillespie is already here, but he's still busy chatting with the other club members. A few minutes ago, Camila, Grace, and I were part of that group, too. We had crowded around a cool new poster listing different types of space rockets and the fuel that powers each of them. We had each picked our favorite and geeked out over the space shuttle that'll be used in the upcoming launch. But when we started a side conversation of our own, we walked over to our seats.

"Oh yeah," says Camila. "I almost forgot about our river plaques. With the rocket launch happening in just a few weeks, it's been hard to concentrate on anything else."

"I haven't gotten an email from anyone yet," I say. "Maybe no one else has, either."

"Didn't you hear?" Grace asks as she scoots her chair closer to me, pausing before continuing. "Someone already got an email from the person who found their board."

This is the most exciting news. I do a little bounce in my seat. "Really? Where was it found? Did the email say how far it traveled?"

Grace must notice a spot on her squeaky-clean glasses lens, because she's wiping them with a soft cloth she's grabbed from her backpack. "I heard it got to the next county over or something," she answers.

"No way," I say, totally impressed.

I'm not sure if Camila is still listening to me and Grace or if she's tuned back into Mr. Gillespie's group conversation until she asks Grace, "Wait, did Connor tell you that?"

Grace narrows her eyes as if trying to read the fine print of her memory. "Connor told me that he heard it from somebody in his math class."

Camila makes a face. "He loves to tell stories. I heard that's not true."

I sink a little in my seat. I could totally believe Connor would make up something like that. That boy will do almost anything to be the center of attention, even for a few minutes. I glance at him right now, in the group talking to our teacher.

"No one I know received an email yet," Camila says with a sigh. She's sitting across from us, so we can see her eyes darting back and forth between us and Mr. Gillespie's conversation. It's like she doesn't want to miss anything happening anywhere.

A small cheer breaks out from the group talking to Mr. Gillespie, but I don't catch why. I think I'm the only one not paying attention to their conversation now, because before I know it, Grace and Camila chime in.

"He shops at the same grocery store my mom does," Grace calls out.

"He's come into my dad's bakery before," adds Camila. "I wasn't there, but my dad told me the whole story."

"Wait, who is everyone talking about?" I ask.

"The lead astronaut on the upcoming NASA launch, Miss Roberts," answers Mr. Gillespie, shooing the excited students over to their seats. Henry grabs the last seat at our table . . . right across from me. I smile at him—and then at Camila and Grace, too—so Henry doesn't get the idea my sudden smile was just for him.

"What else is there for anyone to talk about?" Connor scoffs. "The launch is only the most exciting thing to happen here since the last launch ages ago."

Camila bobs her head in agreement. For her to back up something Connor says has to mean she's pretty pumped about the launch, too, and I don't blame her one bit. I reach out and give her a high five in a mini celebration. Now I totally get why she's been so distracted these past few minutes.

Getting excited about a rocket launch is a requirement for everybody who's breathing in this town. I know people all across the country—and the world—are stoked about it, too, but I've gotta think the most excited ones have got to be the folks here in Cape Canaveral. NASA is in our backyard, so we are all raised with rocket ships in our sightlines. We're so gaga over rocket ships, our area code is even 321!

Plus, rocket science is kind of in my DNA, thanks to my scientist dad. My friends can still hardly believe what he does for a living. They're always begging me for details about his job at NASA, but I can't really say what he's working on for this launch. In fact, I don't know anything more about the launch than anyone else does. Believe me, I've tried to find out, but all it gets me is Dad's standard line:

I can't share every last detail with you, sweetie, and I can't be distracted because I'm up against a deadline.

So yes, to say I'm excited about all this is putting it lightly. But what my dad needs now is for me to play it cool and not be some overexcited kid asking him a million questions. I also need to do the same at school by not spreading any theories or rumors about the launch to my classmates—not that I know any. My dad has been *really* secretive about the details.

But at least I have something new to focus my energy on! Working on going green at home has sparked an idea I can't wait to share with the science club today.

"Before we get started, a couple of quick announcements," says Mr. Gillespie as he finally makes his way to the front of the room. Surprisingly, he pulls a dry-erase marker out of his lab coat pocket and not a piece of candy. Usually, he'd be snacking on some sweet treat by now.

"We have not yet landed on our science-club-in-action project. Every year, we're expected to elevate everyday life at JFK Middle School with at least one scientific advancement constructed and conducted by our fine fellowship here. A reminder that this decision needs to be finalized by our next meeting."

"What happened to our school app idea?" asks Shep. "I thought we were going to team up with the app developers who are coming to town."

"The convention they were all flying in for has been canceled," answers Mr. Gillespie.

Now's my chance to share *my* idea.

"What if . . . ," I blurt out so suddenly, I forget to raise my hand.

Camila raises her eyebrows, and she leans toward me as if anticipating what I have to say. Her eyes are so wide, I almost want to lean back from them.

"What if we work on something that raises environmental awareness? Our field trip inspired me to try and reduce waste at home, so I thought it might be fun to tackle a green project together here, too. We could invite Ms. Gordon from Camp Go Green to come and help us create a garden at the school, like the one we helped harvest."

Camila drops her eyes as if something I said disappointed her.

Connor snickers and nudges Shep with his elbow. "And then we, like, what, give away the food?"

"Actually," I interject. "You may be onto something, Connor."

"I am?" he asks, stunned. But then he recovers. "I mean—I am."

"Yes," I continue, too lost in my thoughts to worry about Camila's expression. She doesn't seem impressed with my idea, but I'm on a roll and can't

be bothered to wonder why. "We can see if they can use the food in our cafeteria."

"Or we can sell the food at the farmers' market on Saturdays," says Henry. "It's held here, on campus, so it would be easy to transport the vegetables. And we could either donate the money we earn to a good cause or save it for our next project."

"A school garden would be amazing," says Grace, swiping at her bangs.

"I actually did have fun in the camp's garden," admits Connor, of all people.

Shep also gives a nonchalant thumbs-up.

Surprised, I look at Camila to see if she'll back us up, but she's avoiding eye contact with me. It's like all the buzz and excitement she built up about the NASA launch seems to have tired her out.

Mr. Gillespie pops the top off his dry-erase marker and scribbles my idea on the whiteboard.

"I'm impressed you all agreed on something so quickly. That means we can get started as soon as Ms. Reimer approves a location for the garden."

I'm pumped everyone is on board with my idea, but I'm confused as to why Camila doesn't seem as jazzed about it. As JFK Middle's elected community outreach officer, I should have something in my toolkit to get Camila excited about this project. But if I can't, I bet Ms. Gordon can. I volunteer to email Ms. Gordon. I'll invite her to visit our school and ask if she'll help us set up our school garden. Fingers crossed she'll say yes.

If everything works out, I can take on Project Go Green at home and Project *Grow* Green at school. Healthier planet, here we come!

Chapter 6

"**A**re you sure you want to touch that without gloves?" Sam asks me as I reach for the trash lid.

It's Saturday morning, and my best friend is leaning against the doorframe of the house instead of stepping into my garage, looking at me like I have flies buzzing around my head.

I feel like reminding Sam my parents keep a pretty tidy garage. There's even a cute workshop in one corner. All the tools are lined neatly in drawers or on wall hooks. Aside from the cobwebs that have formed in tucked-away corners over the years, there's nothing gross about this space.

"Aren't you going to come in here?" I ask.

"You don't need another person in there crowding you," teases Sam. "There are already so many trash bags around." She pinches her nose and presses the button to the automatic garage door.

The sun bathes the garage with light, and the stuffy garbage air begins to floats out, while the fragrant outdoor air floats in.

"I hope that helps," calls out Sam from her safe, clean perch.

I nod and flash her a thumbs-up. It helps more than I expected. Except Sam still doesn't join me in the garage.

"What?" she asks, as if reading my mind. "The air may have changed, but the number of trash bags around you hasn't."

We both laugh. I guess I really will be digging in these bags of garbage on my own.

I've kept my asks for my family to a minimum. Tossing their personal trash into the bin with their name on it is all they had to do.

But I can't believe how many bags of trash my family has after just one week.

Luckily, I have Sam to help me sort through it (even if just from afar). She was reluctant to do this when I first called to ask for her help. But now Sam

is really taking her Go Green team volunteer work seriously. She organizes the trash-census chart and tallies what's been thrown away as I call out everything I sift through.

We start with Marie's bin and trash bags.

"What? Three pairs of jeans?" Sam's mouth hangs open when she sees what I've pulled out.

I heave out a sigh and shake my head. "With all the fashionable stuff my sister creates with her sewing machine, I don't understand why she couldn't do something with these."

"Well, they do look super old-fashioned."

"But isn't retro cool?" I ask, not falling for Sam's argument one second.

"Yes, retro is cool, but old-fashioned is . . . old-fashioned."

"Moving on," I say.

Sam scribbles down everything we see in Marie's bin—a few sheets of loose-leaf paper, plastic makeup packaging, and lots of plastic coffee cups and straws.

"Do your mom's bin next," says Sam, playing the back seat driver. I chuckle at her being super eager, but not eager enough to come closer.

"Okay, drumroll," I say, lifting the lid.

Sam beats on the doorframe a little too hard. "Ouch!" She examines her fingernail.

"Okay, no drumroll." I grin and then pull out a plastic bag full of packing peanuts.

"Uh, is there a plastic elephant in the room that we're not talking about?"

"No, my mom's just been going *nutty* with deliveries. She's got more of them coming in than usual." I look at the recycling bin in the corner of the garage where my mom has folded the broken-down delivery boxes neatly.

"Anything else in there?" Sam asks.

I pull out a few take-out containers, plastic uten-sils, and a mountain of crumpled paper. Sam makes a note of all of this.

"Last but not least, my dad," I say, whipping open the bin's lid. I start sifting through the bag on top. "A few junk-food wrappers, balled-up paper, shred-ded paper, torn paper, and a pretty good amount of plastic water bottles."

"Got it," says Sam, her pen moving quickly as she jots down everything.

"Wow, going through those bags didn't give me the boost I'd expected," I say. "My family's habits are in worse shape than I thought."

"Well, maybe a Grace-inspired color-coordinated census will cheer you up," says Sam, joking about our chart-loving friend. "We'll give each individual partic-ipant a color code, to make everything easier to track."

I smile and nod. Sam is over-the-top in the best possible way. It must be an actor-and-dancer thing, but everything she does has flair.

"Of course, *you* would find a way to give trash personality," I tease her.

Sam shrugs with a giggle.

☺🌳🍾

After Sam leaves—our color-coded trash census completed—I do a sweep of the house to see what other things my family might need to work on in phase two of our Go Green project.

I peek into Marie's and my parents' rooms, and then I do a walk-through of the living room and the kitchen. Some lights are on, power strips aren't turned off, and the dishwasher is ready to run half-full, plus disposable coffee cups and crushed bottles of water are in the trash. Once I've completed my observations, I zip through the house, hitting "off" switches, tossing disposable cups and bottles into the recycling bin, and reloading the dishwasher. I gather all the plastic grocery bags and hang washed clothes on the new clothesline I set up in the backyard.

Next, I dig out all the coffee thermoses and reusable water bottles I can find in the cupboards and line them on the kitchen counter so my family won't forget to grab them on their way out the door. I leave a piece of scrap paper with *TAKE ONE* written across it in front of the bottles, just in case it's not obvious to anyone what they're for.

I also pull out reusable tote bags where everyone can find them, and I place one of my extra dry-erase boards on Dad's desk so he can use that instead of

Project Go Green
Phase 2

Grab a reusable bottle and
a reusable bag on your way out.

Hang clothes out to dry.
(P.S. See new clothesline in backyard.)

Limit your printing.

Turn off unnecessary lights/ power strips.

Gather old clothes for donation.

Keep tracking your trash!

so much paper. The glass jars I pull out of the trash bins can totally be repurposed as vases or maybe even collection jars.

Last but not least, I create a phase-two list and tack it on the fridge. This way, it will be easy for my family to remember the little changes they're supposed to be making throughout the day.

- Grab a reusable bottle and a reusable bag on your way out.
- Hang clothes out to dry. (P.S. See new clothesline in backyard.)
- Limit your printing.
- Turn off unnecessary lights / power strips.
- Gather old clothes for donation.
- Keep tracking your trash!

🌍🦋🍷

When everyone gathers for dinner that evening, I catch their attention. Mom's brought home takeout (again), and Dad and Marie plan to grab their portion and run off to eat and work in the office and in the backyard.

Clinking my fork against my glass tumbler draws three pairs of eyes to me. Cosmo and Rocket perk up, too.

"Before you all head out, I just want to take a quick moment to let you know how the trash census is going," I start, holding up the color-coordinated poster.

Marie takes a sip of the iced-coffee cup she always seems to have, and Dad pops a large corn chip into his mouth.

"Sure, honey," says Mom when no one else reacts. The crunch sound of Dad's sneaky snack isn't as muffled as he likely thinks it is.

I nod at her in appreciation. "We are entering phase two of our Go Green project. Based on our trash audit, Sam and I have created this chart to track and break down everyone's individual waste. To make things easier for you, I'll have reusable cups and reusable bags lined up on the counter every day. All you have to do is grab them. Also, if you have time, there's a list of additional things we can all be doing posted on the fridge to help keep us on track." I point toward the list I tacked up earlier today.

I look at my audience, waiting for a response. Marie's mouth is full, but she gives me a thumbs-up as she makes a beeline for the back patio.

"Sounds good," says Dad before he disappears down

the hall. Mom opens her mouth to respond, but she's interrupted by a loud muffled ringing. Her phone must be buried in her purse somewhere. She rushes to her room to spill out her bag and take the call.

"Go team?" I say weakly to myself. There's no response, other than closing doors and Mom's ringtone.

Sure, getting my family to do their part may be frustrating, but as Ms. Gordon says, "The earth is worth it." Besides, if Galaxy Girl can save the universe, I can help save my own planet—right?

Chapter 7

One look at my email before school, and I do a happy dance. Rocket hears my private celebration and runs into my room to help me bust some moves. I grab her front legs, and we do our favorite *Dancing with the Paws* routine. As big and mopey

as she can be sometimes, Rocket is my favorite dance partner.

I laugh so hard, I can't keep our two-step move going. Cosmo hears the commotion and trots to the door to see what we're doing. He takes one look, then seems to shake his head before turning tail and leaving.

"You don't even know what we're celebrating, you big lug," I tell Rocket, who clearly doesn't mind. Her tongue hangs out like she doesn't need to have any more info.

"Well, I'm going to tell you anyway. We're celebrating because Ms. Gordon emailed me back. She said she can come to our science club this week!"

Blank doggy stare.

"Don't you know what that means? Our school garden will get the best head start."

Getting a yes from Ms. Gordon is the good news I needed.

🌍🌳🍷

"Imitation is the best form of flattery," Grace says with a smirk when she looks up from her tablet screen. We're at our usual cafeteria table, and I've just shown Grace a pic of the color-coordinated chart Sam and I created in her honor.

"If that's true, then how come no one has brought in tasty desserts for *me* to try?" Camila chuckles.

"We got you something from the vending machine

just yesterday," I tease Camila. Grace and I laugh at the unimpressed way she looks at us.

"You're welcome." Grace grins.

Camila finally breaks character and laughs.

"But seriously, this looks good, Hope," says Grace. "Is the Roberts family Go Green project going well, then?"

"Actually, if it weren't for Sam, I'd be a Green Team of one," I say. "Everyone has been too preoccupied to do more than the bare minimum."

"I'm sure your dad must be super busy with all the launch planning," says Camila, her eyes wide with interest. "And we need him to stay focused so that everything can go amazing on launch day!" Camila leans in and asks me, "Has he been to meetings with the astronauts? Do they *know* him? I wonder if they know if they'll do a space walk during this mission. Does your dad know?"

My head is spinning from all of Camila's questions. They're the same questions that have been swirling in my mind, too. I wish I knew the answers, but my dad hasn't been sharing. Thinking about how long it's been since I've had a good gab fest with Dad makes me feel sad. Camila is waiting for me to

answer, though, so I bring up another piece of exciting news instead.

"We've got our own launch to worry about on *this* planet," I say. "Ms. Gordon is coming Friday to get us started on our garden. Are you guys ready to work the earth?"

At this, Grace gives a little cheer, but Camila barely cracks a smile.

🌍🥦🌱

Later that week, we learn that not only did Ms. Reimer approve of our garden plot, she also donated enough gardening gloves for everyone in science club. I almost wear them to meet Ms. Gordon, but then I decide that would be a tad bit extra.

"Ms. Gordon, it's great to see you again!" I greet my favorite camp counselor when I see her standing at the office's front desk. She's just signed in as a JFK Middle guest.

"I was so pleased you invited me to come," she says.

Ms. Gordon looks different outside of a log cabin or the natural sunlight. The fluorescent lighting overhead almost makes it seem like I'm looking at her through a cell phone screen and not in person.

"It must be tough being away from the forest," I say, wondering if Ms. Gordon feels out of place.

Ms. Gordon winks and smiles at me. "Well, you know, even though I love the forest critters, I'm still a human, so places like this are my habitat, too."

"Oh, right," I say, slightly embarrassed, even though it *is* fun hearing Ms. Gordon's unique words of wisdom again.

"I hear I'm in for a tour?" she asks.

"Yes, and I'm honored to be the one who gets to show you around our school." I hold the front office door open for her to walk through. Mr. G. asked me to take some time showing Ms. Gordon around while the science club unpacks the shipment of gardening seeds and tools that have finally come in and gets set up outside.

Ms. Gordon makes an awesome guest, and she seems really interested in hearing about JFK Middle's history of successful alumni, like my mom. Not surprisingly, she spends the most time admiring the school's outdoor spaces. My favorite moment of the tour is when she playfully growls as she takes a picture with the tiger mascot statue in the grand entryway.

But the best part is, Ms. Gordon answers all of my burning questions. I hope I'm not bugging her, but there's so much I'm curious to know. After asking her about her time working in the Smoky Mountains, I turn my questions to matters closer to home.

"Even with me trying to make it easy for them, I didn't think it would be this tough to get my family to reduce waste. Is there a trick to changing their habits?"

"I wish I knew the answer to that," Ms. Gordon answers. "But one thing I've learned is that you have to ease people into making changes, not guilt them into it."

"I'll remember that," I sigh.

"Your good example will show them that small changes can lead to bigger changes over time. It sounds like you're doing all the right things with your trash census," continues Ms. Gordon. "Small acts every day can make an impact. Keep modeling how it's done, and they'll come around."

Ms. Gordon and I are still chatting when we get to the outdoor plot of our future school garden. Mr. Gillespie and my fellow members of the science club seem to instantly let down their guard when they see Ms. Gordon's beaming face.

Everyone welcomes her with so much excitement. Grace, Camila, Henry, Ezra, Shep, and even Connor all shout out their greetings.

"Hey, Ms. Gordon!" says Grace.

"Welcome to our neck of the woods!" greets Henry.

Connor doesn't miss a beat. "Ahem—pun intended."

"Aw, thank you, thank you. You guys are too sweet," says Ms. Gordon, pausing to take in everyone's faces. "So, where do I pitch my tent for the night?"

Camila looks worried. "You're not expecting us to sleep out here . . . are you?"

"Gotcha!" Ms. Gordon laughs, and Mr. Gillespie grins along with her.

Ezra shakes his head. "Even though there are no bears around here, I'd still be afraid to camp outside overnight."

"You'd be surprised how much making it through the night helps you overcome those fears," Ms. Gordon says as she pulls out a pair of gardening gloves from her bag. She's come prepared. "You go from feeling uncomfortable to powerful. Just like with the night hike, we have to learn how to push through our discomforts. If more people were comfortable in natural spaces, we'd all feel more responsible for helping these spaces thrive."

I nod and imagine how heroic I'd feel just waking up in the wild the next morning after conquering my fear the night before.

"And as for bears, they're mostly harmless," Ms. Gordon continues. "My best bear sighting was watching a mother black bear and her two cubs cross the road right in front of my tour Jeep. I had to slam on the brakes when I saw the mama, and then two adorable cubs ran right behind her. One of the cubs lost them after they ran into the bush of

the forest, so she climbed up a tree and then slid down like a firefighter on a pole when she finally spotted her family."

"That's such a great story," I say, touching my hand to my heart.

"Aw, black bears are the cutest," Camila coos. It's good to see her enjoying Ms. Gordon's visit, because she hasn't seemed that thrilled when I've mentioned the garden over the last week. I've been meaning to talk to her about it, but I've been so busy with my Project Go Green, I haven't had the chance to find out why.

Today, at least, Camila looks interested in Ms. Gordon's presentation on the benefits of a school garden. As Ms. Gordon shares important information about the best placement for each veggie we're planting, she's working the garden tools in the earth. We watch and listen closely as she demonstrates how to keep the soil healthy and shares some optimum ways to make the most of the plot space we have.

We spend the next hour digging, planting, labeling, hauling, and repeating everything again. We plant all types of seeds in the earth—tomatoes, carrots, radishes, zucchini, and more. Our clothes get dirty, but no one seems to mind one bit.

Before our meeting comes to a close, Ms. Gordon offers to answer any questions, and a few hands go up.

"I'm still not understanding how gardening helps the environment," Shep admits. "Can you explain that again?"

"Eating locally grown produce means you rely less on it being transported in, which means less trucks on the road and less emissions in the air. Also, less packaging to trash."

Shep nods. "I never thought of it that way."

Ms. Gordon points at Grace next.

"Are school gardens this large a thing, because I've never heard of any other schools doing this."

"Oh, sure," answers

Ms. Gordon, her long braids swaying with her hand gestures. "There are *lots* of organizations that work hard to help schools set up gardens. They know that gardens not only help the environment but also help students with nutrition, outdoor exercise, and gaining an understanding of nature's cycles."

"I love that!" I shout, even more excited that we got JFK Middle on board.

After Ms. Gordon answers a few more questions, Camila squeezes one last one in.

"Do you come to Cape Canaveral often?" Camila asks.

"No, it's actually my first time here," Ms. Gordon confesses.

Hearing this makes me feel bad about taking up so much of the tour with my own questions.

But when Camila asks her follow-up question, it isn't anywhere close to what I expected.

"Did you know that our whole town is eagerly looking forward to NASA's rocket launch in two weeks?"

"Yes, I've been reading up on the details. You are all so lucky to have a front-row seat to these events!"

"I'm going to try to get tickets to the on-site viewing," brags Connor.

"There's no way you can get those tickets unless you signed up for them a year ago," counters Shep.

"You don't know that—" Connor gets out before Mr. Gillespie cuts him off.

"Future scientists, we are here to discuss the science of environmentalism. Now, if there are no further questions, I'm sure Ms. Gordon will need to start her trip back home."

"Thank you. I'm glad you found this presentation so helpful," Ms. Gordon says, an amused look on her face. "I have a feeling you young people are going to leave the earth way better than you found it."

After our science club meeting ends, Camila,

Grace, and I walk Ms. Gordon back to the front office. She tells us more stories about close encounters with animals in the forest.

"You should have your own TV show," says Camila. "We've learned so much from you."

"Yeah," adds Grace. "As far as I can tell, not many women host nature shows."

"If you get scouted, Grace will probably offer to be your manager," teases Camila.

"I can vouch for her—she really is the best manager you can ask for." I grin.

That amused look is back on Ms. Gordon's face as she thanks us. After Ms. Gordon signs out at the front office, Grace and Camila head home, and I walk Ms. Gordon to the entrance to see her off.

When Ms. Gordon points out her car across the parking lot, I'm not surprised to see it's electric and eco-friendly.

"It's all about reducing emissions. Better for the environment. Better for your lungs!"

As I watch her car quietly pull away without the puff of gray smoke a lot of cars and school buses burp out, I wonder how bad the air quality around the school must be. And the carpool and bus lanes are on the same side of the school as the garden. Will that affect the health of our produce?

That's it.

The science club should test the air quality around the school and make changes to reduce the pollution!

Mr. Gillespie and the rest of the science club might groan at the extra work when I bring this up, but if this is something we can do to pitch in, we should. Why wait for another year or another group project when we are equipped to help *now*? Plus, cleaner air means healthier—and yummier—veggies. Besides, the earth *is* worth it.

Chapter 8

That night, before I head to bed, I wash my family's water bottles and thermoses and line them up clean on the counter. Even though tomorrow is Saturday, my mom and sister will be out early for appointments and errands. Hopefully, they remember to grab their bottles this time. They've been forgetting all week and then apologizing later. It's always the same excuse, about how they're too busy to keep up with these changes.

When I get up the next morning, all the bottles and thermoses are lined up right where I left them. Seeing this bums me out. I decide that today, I'm going to let them know how I'm feeling.

I'm in the garage later that afternoon counting trash bags in the bins when my mom pulls into her parking spot.

"Hi, honey," Mom greets me with a warm smile.

Marie unfolds herself out of the passenger seat and gives me a lazy wave.

I turn from the bins to talk to them about what I witnessed inside. "Hey, Mom, Marie . . . I noticed—" But they both have already slipped inside. Yup, just that fast. We don't even get the chance to make eye contact before they run off to chip away at their busy to-do lists.

I puff out a huge sigh, and not just because the trash is kind of stinky.

I head indoors and find them both in the kitchen, surrounded by Rocket and Cosmo, who are running circles around their ankles. Marie is leaning against the counter, right in front of the bottles I've lined up for everyone. "Did you guys notice anything?" I ask with a *ta-da* tone to my voice.

My mom squeezes my shoulder on her way down the hall. "Oh, yeah," she replies absentmindedly. "Thank you for taking out the trash, honey. I know it gets pretty stinky near the bins. I'll be in my bedroom if anyone needs me."

Marie never notices the line of bottles, but she looks up from her phone to flash me a quizzical look. "What's gotten into you?" she asks.

I push aside my disappointment and focus on how nice it is my big sister's noticed I have something to say. So, I come out with it.

"In the trash audit, we realized just how many disposable bottles and cups our family throws away," I start. "I dug up and washed out the reusable water bottles and thermoses for you guys to take each morning, but you're always forgetting them or leaving them behind. I figured taking a thermos with you to the coffee shop would be a simple task you could do each day, until it becomes routine. We need to get in the habit of making these small changes so that we can move on to bigger ones."

"Ew, sorry I asked," Marie jokes. Her smirk almost makes me smile back, but I don't. I want her to take this seriously.

I fold my arms and then unfold them. Is that all she's going to say? I can feel any appreciation for Marie's check-in fading away.

"Look, if it's that important to you, it's important to us," she finally says. "It's a busy time now, but we'll work on it. Just keep leaving them on the counter, and if we forget to grab one by mistake, have a little patience."

Marie's phone dings, and in the next millisecond, her eyes are back to being glued to her screen. She almost trips over Cosmo on her way out of the kitchen.

"Okay, I'll be patient," I say. "But if you don't look where you're walking, you'll *be* a patient."

That makes both me and Marie chuckle, which helps. And when she takes her video-chat call to the backyard, I decide that a walk with the dogs will help me cool off even more.

As I double back to my room to get my phone, I look at the closed office door. Dad has been in there all morning, giving off a

strong do-not-disturb vibe. My knuckles are itching to knock on the door, and I even walk over to it and let my hand dangle high in the air. But as soon as I hear an exasperated sigh, I think twice of it and back away quietly.

I close my eyes, knowing that this Dad shutout will be another bummed-out thought I'll have to walk off. I walk it off all the way to the beachside dog park. After tossing sticks at Cosmo and Rocket a few times, I take a seat and watch them play with other dogs.

When I get back home over an hour later, I'm determined to stay positive. Sure, my family keeps forgetting about the reusable bottles. But at least our trash bins at our curb aren't overflowing like they were last week. That's because so much of our waste actually belonged in the recycling bin. It took me an hour to sort that all out, but I did. And, of course, it was frustrating doing it all on my own. And yes, I might have to stay up later to get my homework done on trash night. But I'm glad to do it. We all have to make some minor sacrifices to protect the earth.

And maybe I'm not the only one making them. When I go in the kitchen, the clean bottles aren't there. And I'm really blown away to see my dad heading to the grocery store carrying a stack of reusable bags.

Finally, a sign of progress. Bigger changes, here we come!

Chapter 9

"**D**oesn't that sound like the best idea?" I ask, not expecting to get an answer. It's Monday morning, and I'm all alone in my science class. I'm well aware this is a one-way conversation with the classroom poster of Albert Einstein. But I like to think he somehow answers me back with a feeling.

"Did you just wink at Albert Einstein?" Camila enters the room and settles into her seat next to mine.

"Camila, any louder and you'll have the whole school thinking Einstein's been feeding me answers to Mr. G.'s pop quizzes."

We both snicker at the silliness of the thought.

"That's one thing we know that Einstein doesn't do," Camila says.

"What, the science of gossip spreading?" I joke.

Camila grins, but the corners of her mouth start to slide down and melt into a frown. "Einstein never got to know space travel." She pauses. "Don't you think that's kind of sad?"

I nod. "I never thought of that before, but you have a point," I admit.

"It makes me think of what rad advancements in science *we'll* miss," says Camila.

"Girl, if we miss the discovery of real-life super-heroes, or if someone invents a flying cape, and I miss out on the possibility of actually *becoming* a superhero, I don't know if I could get over that," I say. I'm only halfway teasing, but it still makes Camila snap out of her mood and smile.

Mr. Gillespie hasn't come into class yet, but I admit, I'm eager to pitch him my new science club idea. When he finally walks in, he mumbles something about a jammed teachers' lounge printer and starts handing out pop quiz sheets right away.

Before we get started, Camila and I both give Einstein an exaggerated wink, just in case.

Sam likes to call me a Science MVP, because she can't see how a pop quiz is a good thing. But here, in our Advanced Science class, there's no better way to boost our moods.

By the time class is over, a lot of us have a bounce in our steps as we leave class. I tell Camila I'll catch up with her, and I stay behind to chat with Mr. Gillespie about the eco-friendly idea sparked by Ms. Gordon's visit last Friday.

Surprisingly, it doesn't take much to convince Mr. Gillespie to get behind running an air-quality

test on campus. "I appreciate the garden idea—it's different than anything the science club has ever done—but I did wish we had chosen something more school-wide. Air-quality tests would certainly impact the entire school."

"That's great! Then can I pitch it to the club on Friday?" I ask, ready to launch faster than a NASA rocket.

"Yes, but first"—Mr. Gillespie leans back as if he's pulling the reins on my hastiness—"you need to consult Vice Principal Reimer. We can't do this without her okay, since she'll need to alert bus drivers and parents to avoid disrupting the experiment."

"Yes, sir, Mr. G." Awkwardly, I give him a salute before I can stop myself. Nothing to do now but to recover with a joke. "I'll get Ms. Reimer's *green* light for this *green* project."

Mr. Gillespie's lips stretch into a thin line, and he raises one eyebrow. Somebody's not in a joking mood. I guess giving a pop quiz isn't as fun as taking one.

"That's no problem," I say without the fun in my tone. "I'll do that after school and report back to you tomorrow." On my way out of his classroom, I look back at Mr. G., and I'm not surprised he's already leafing through our pop quizzes.

⊙❀♀

Vice Principal Reimer and I have history. I've had to visit her office a few times to get approvals for fund-raisers and for campaign ideas when I was running for class president.

At the dismissal bell, I hurry to the front office so I can make her visiting hours before anyone else gets there.

"Why, hello, Miss Roberts," Ms. Reimer says as she invites me into her office. "It's been, what, almost a month? I was beginning to wonder how you're managing without me."

Unlike Mr. G., Ms. Reimer seems in a more cheerful mood. She wordlessly hands me a watering can and gestures at her mini jungle of houseplants lining the windowsills, walls, desks, and end tables.

"I'm glad you're available. I was sure someone would already be waiting to talk with you by now," I say.

"Well, thank you for making me sound so popular," Ms. Reimer says with a hint of a smile. "Let's look at it more like you have great timing."

"Right, no, of course," I stammer. "I totally didn't mean it that way."

If I want to get Ms. Reimer's okay for our newest green project, I could at least try not insulting her.

I decide to jump straight to the big ask, so I don't risk any more mistakes. "The science club would like your permission to run air-quality tests in the carpool and bus lane areas."

"I see. Does this have anything to do with the new garden that's located nearby?" she asks, leafing through a tall stack of books at the edge of her desk. She stops to pat the top of her head, I assume in search of her glasses.

"They're around your neck," I tell Ms. Reimer, who looks down and spies her glasses dangling like a necklace.

"Oh, right, thank you," she says, placing her specs on her face to look closer at the book she's been holding open.

"The garden plot borders Building A," I continue, using the official building names straight from the student guidebook, as an added touch and reminder that I've done my homework. "The air quality there is a concern, yes, but these high-traffic areas are also close to the school entrances. That means fumes can get into the school and that our students and staff aren't getting a break from inhaling them."

Ms. Reimer listens as I talk, but she's only half paying attention. She's more focused on finding some passage in the book she's been scanning. Her fingers slide down every page with increasing speed.

I clear my throat and speak up louder, explaining the details of the plan. We would test the areas closest to the doors to find out whether fumes can be detected there. Next, we'd test the garden area and closer to the carpool and bus lanes.

As I speak, Ms. Reimer actually looks up at me.

"Interesting," she says over and over as I drop a few facts on the dangers of carbon emissions, even in an open-air area like the entrance corner of our school. "I've always wondered about that."

"Well, a few simple tests and we can have those answers for you soon after we start collecting the data we need."

Silence. No immediate response, and I wonder if I've said too much. Marie is right. She's always telling me I don't have to spill all the fun facts I know in one sitting. I wait silently for Ms. Reimer's answer.

"I'll look forward to hearing the air-quality results and proposed solutions once the science club has that information," she says.

This is the best news! I feel like running back to

the lab to announce our green light to Mr. G., but with no science club going on after school, he's probably already gone for the day. "Thank you, Ms. Reimer! From me and the earth." I flash my amused vice principal a confident smile.

"The science club and I are on the case!"

Chapter 10

Something smells so amazing. Before I even step inside my house, the aroma of a home-cooked meal beckons to me from the front walkway. Sam and her mom have just dropped me off—my parents have been working late all week, so I've been catching the school bus or getting rides from Sam's mom—and I can't wait to find out what this is all about.

Cosmo and Rocket greet me at the door, like they want to be the ones to tell me about my family's planned dinner surprise: delicious salmon cakes glazed in a yummy sauce and served with garlic mashed potatoes and spinach avocado salad.

I never expected to see this entire spread. And so early in the evening? That's a first.

"Our final guest has arrived," says Dad. I run off to wash my hands, and when I return, Dad pulls out a chair for me in grand style.

Mom and Marie are adding the finishing touches to the table, but they grin at Dad's fancy gesture.

I slip into my chair and start pouring water from a pitcher into each person's tumbler. This is the first night in a long time we haven't ordered takeout for dinner. Could work demands finally be slowing down for my family?

"I can't believe we are all sitting down together enjoying a home-cooked meal," I say to the three faces—Mom, Dad, and Marie—gathered around our kitchen table. I get a sudden urge to check the counter to see if the reusable bottles and thermoses are still lined up where I put them this morning, or if the trash is overflowing again with the scraps from dinner prep, but I don't do it. It'll spoil the mood if they are, and I just want to enjoy this moment.

"Get ready for the tastiest meal you've had in weeks!" says Dad, rubbing his hands together like the lovable goofball he is.

I turn to look at my amazing mom. "Thank you for doing this. It all looks incredible."

"How do you know Mom was the one who cooked this?" Dad asks, curling his lower lip out to curry extra sympathy.

"Aw, I'm so sorry." I backpedal my last statement. "Wow, Dad, you outdid yourself."

The salmon cakes are the perfect grade of crispy. Dad must've used our new air fryer.

Marie drops her fork with a clang to her plate. "Hey, now I'm offended," she says with an even poutier pout. "You assumed Dad made this but didn't ask me."

"Ohmygosh, Marie, I didn't mean to assume—" I pause and look at all the grinning going on without me. "Wait a minute. Are you all messing with me?"

Everyone cracks up.

"Hope, baby, thank you for your compliment," says Mom finally. "I'm glad you love the dinner I alone made."

Dad and Marie clear their throats. *"Ahem!"*

"With a little help," says Mom. She holds up her hand, showing a tiny bit of space between her thumb and index finger.

Now it's my turn to laugh. Cosmo and Rocket run up to me with their tails wagging when I do. Maybe they're counting on some of my food to accidentally fall from my mouth.

"So, no planning meetings going on for you tonight, Mom?" Marie asks once the table has settled down from all the joking around.

"We're meeting at the crack of dawn tomorrow morning," she says with a sigh. "Hence, the super-early dinner tonight."

My mother has been hosting one meeting after another both at her gallery and virtually from home. Being in charge of this citywide public arts

project is a huge deal. Just like the rocket launch, our entire town is excited about it. People usually know the exact date each year when the city arts theme will be announced. I can't remember another year, though, when the theme has been decided on this late.

"Any idea on what the theme is going to be?" I ask Mom.

"I loved when you guys installed artsy pianos all over town a few years ago," recalls Marie.

"Oh yeah! The bright yellow one by Woolly Pier was my favorite," I say.

Mom gives a smiling nod at the memory. "The

artists we commissioned had so much fun with that one," she says. "I wish we were as sure about the theme this year as we were back then. There's barely two weeks before announcement day, and so far, no proposed idea is knocking my socks off."

"It'll come to you, honey," says Dad, giving my mom's hand a gentle pat. "It always does."

"Look on the bright side," adds Marie. "Everyone's so excited by the rocket launch, the town will be deliriously happy about whatever you decide!"

Mom throws back her head and sighs. "Boy, I hope so."

"Are kids in your school super distracted about the launch, too?" I ask.

Marie's eyes widen. "Super."

I lean toward my dad as much as I can without falling out of my chair. "If only we had some inside info we could share with them."

"Oh, right," teases Marie. "But where, oh where would we get that kind of knowledge?"

"Very funny, you two," says Dad. "You know I would share if I could."

I wipe my mouth to cover my frown. Marie and I know all too well that Dad has a particular way of working at times like these. He usually keeps his head down and doesn't say much about whatever project he's working on until he's feeling less overwhelmed. He just prefers it that way. So we try to avoid asking him about work until he's cleared his deadlines and can come out of his cave again.

I've been keeping up with all the reports about this new mission on my favorite space-travel website, but I do miss hearing Dad's firsthand updates about upgrades that are being made to the spaceship. And I miss talking about space stuff with Camila, without the pressure of her wanting the inside scoop.

What I miss even more, though, is just being able to talk with Dad. Dad must know how excited I am about this launch, but he's not acting like he does. He's been so busy I've barely seen him for longer than it takes to scarf down a meal. And he hasn't been up for our epic chats these days, either—even to talk about nonwork stuff. At least the new science club garden and handling all the Project Go Green stuff at home have been a good way to distract myself.

"Yes, we know you would tell us about the mission if you could, Dad," says Marie. I'm jealous she's able to be so mature about things. I understand, but I still can't help but feel a little shut out.

"When things are looking like all systems go, you'll be the first ones I'll tell," Dad says.

I give Dad a little smile, but I can't help thinking, for once, I wish the rocket launch was already over.

Chapter 11

On Friday afternoon at the start of our science club meeting, Mr. Gillespie invites me to share my latest news with the class. I stand and pivot so that I'm facing everyone in the room.

"You've all received an email about the air-quality tests," I start, a part of me a little nervous even though my friends seemed to like the idea when I first told them about it. "As you know, Ms. Reimer has signed off on us conducting these tests on JFK Middle's carpool and bus lanes. She updated me that she's informed everyone this will be happening, which means we can officially get started today!"

"Awesome, another green light," Henry calls out. "Let's floor it!"

"Yay!" I squeal and go airborne for a half a second.

After that's settled, our members then turn to Grace, our newly appointed project manager, as she takes her place in front of the room. She starts her talk by explaining what we'll need to do to keep on schedule.

"We've now got the school garden and the air-quality test going on simultaneously," gushes Grace. "So it's important we not only make progress at a steady pace, but we stay on task, too."

Grace is totally in her element, just like she was when she was manager of both my and Chloe's campaigns for class president. Anytime a project needs mapping out, Grace is the first to volunteer her amazing planning, scheduling, and graphing skills. She actually has fun collecting data and making prediction models. Grace takes organization to the next level, and I love to see it.

Henry, Connor, and Ezra volunteer to head outside to the garden site and check in on the seedlings we planted with Ms. Gordon during our last meeting.

"I help out with the gardening at home, so this should be easy," Henry had said before leaving the lab with his gloves and a few garden tools in hand.

As for Camila and me, we're leading the charge on the air-quality tests. We set up shop in the far corner of the room and demonstrate for Shep how to program the sensors we'll use to detect air pollution on the school's property.

I hold up the separate parts in the air so we can all see. "These sensors are sensitive to the light found in pollutants," I explain.

Mr. G. comes over and helps me get my facts straight after I trip over some information. It's my first time using a device like this, and there's a lot of new info to remember. This project is important to me, the school, and the planet, so I appreciate Mr. Gillespie's help in making sure it's done right.

"In order for the science club to accurately test air quality, this detector will need to measure the curbside pollution around the school several times each day for over a week," Mr. Gillespie reminds us.

Once our coding group—consisting of Shep and Grace—pulls up their sleeves and starts working on the detectors, Camila and I grab our notebooks and head toward the front of the school to observe the after-school activities there. What we see will help us decide the best air-pollution testing locations.

We walk down the sixth-grade locker area and toward the side doors that lead to the school bus pickup and drop-off area. There are still a few kids grabbing clothes or books from lockers that hint at what everyone's bedrooms at home might look like.

Even though Camila didn't seem excited about our environmentally friendly projects at first, she seems to have come around. Today she's in a great mood. She's practically skipping down the hall, which puts a skip in my step, too.

"How's your dad doing?" Camila asks me.

"Still busy," I answer. "But can you blame him with everything that's going on right now?"

Camila blinks a few times, as if waking up from a daydream. "I know! Just thinking about what we're a part of makes me love STEM even more than I thought possible."

"Science has such an impact on so many parts of our everyday lives. I can't imagine spending a day without it," I say, a little bit too dramatically. But at least I'm being honest.

"Same—and I wouldn't want to. It makes my science heart happy to think about what we're going to witness," confesses Camila.

I hug my notepad closer to me. Camila and I are so engrossed in our conversation, practically nose to nose. "It's going to take a lot of teamwork for everything to go smoothly, but think of how many people will benefit!"

"Hey, you two!" a voice calls out. We look behind us and spot our friends Chloe and Bella.

"Hey, girls!" greets Camila.

Bella rolls up to my side. "What were you guys talking about?"

Camila and I answer her question at the same time.

"Our science club projects," I reply.

"The rocket launch," says Camila.

Wait. What?

Camila and I stare at each other like we're just noticing each other's presence for the first time.

Chloe chuckles. "Um, for two people who looked like you were sharing the same bubble, you guys sure are in two separate orbits."

Bella lifts a sparkly painted fingertip to us. "But I love the sound of either one of those conversations."

Camila and I give both girls weak smiles before they head to find their rides home. I watch them get swallowed up by the sea of skateboard stunt kids, football tossers, bicycle commuters, and other after-school stragglers.

When it's just the two of us standing awkwardly together, we focus on our task.

"I guess one of us can take the school bus zone and the other can check out the carpool lane," I say.

"I'll head to the carpool," Camila offers.

"Cool," I say.

We take off in two different directions and get to work making observations and jotting down notes to share with the science club.

After some note taking, we meet at the side entrance and exchange our findings. Our mood is so much lighter than it was earlier in the hallway. I guess with a little time, it's easier now to laugh at our misunderstanding. Camila and I go over the results, and the most important thing we learn is that the school bus zone is yards closer to the school's entry doors than the carpool zone.

"I guess we should go back to the lab and let everyone know," I say with a slight smile.

"Let's do it," answers Camila.

On our way back inside, we run into Henry, Connor, and Ezra. They've just come from our garden plot.

"How was your cushy fact-finding mission?" asks Connor. "You know, what you were doing while we did the *real* work?" His clothes are smeared with dirt, and he seems kind of proud of it.

"Finally, someone else gets to hear Connor brag

for a change," jokes Ezra, throwing an arm around Connor, who shrugs it off.

"It's not bragging if it's the truth," Connor responds.

"The truth is," says Henry with a smirk, "the garden was a team effort, so we all deserve the credit."

"Well, lie to them all you want," whines Connor. "But all *I* know is I may have found yet another superpower of mine. These green thumbs got the garden sprouting ahead of schedule. It looks like a few lettuce leaves are already budding."

"Hey," I say. "I seem to remember planting some of those lettuce seeds."

"Um, me too," Ezra jokes.

"Nope. If there's no photo, it didn't happen," says Connor, walking ahead to the restroom to wash off. "Meet you guys back at the lab," he says to Ezra and Henry.

As soon as the guys are out of earshot, Camila and I crack up. We laugh at Connor's unexpected gardener sass, we laugh at our misunderstanding, and we laugh at us being silly enough to crack up about it all.

🌍♻️🌳

Right before the science club meeting is over, I ask Mr. Gillespie if I can address the group again.

"Make it quick," he says.

"Being in the science club is not just about doing

experiments and entering science fairs, but about applying science to our own everyday lives," I say. "Visiting Camp Go Green has inspired me in so many ways, and I'm proud of what we're doing to be kinder to our planet and the people who live on it.

"I know a few of you mentioned selling the veggies from our garden at the farmers' market. I wonder if we could consider donating some of our produce to a food bank, too? I pulled together a list of local ones."

"Thank you, Miss Roberts," says Mr. G. "I'll take one of those sheets, if you please."

I gladly hand him and the rest of the science club members copies of the list. Everyone looks them over before bursting out in supportive comments,

and I can't stop my own big grin from bursting out, too.

It feels good knowing that the earth may be getting a few more guardians and protectors.

Chapter 12

The next week, I come to school with a few flyers for the science club's booth at the farmers' market. The veggies are sprouting, so we'll be ready to do our first mini harvest in just a few more weeks. Before lunch, I stop at the new bulletin board in the cafeteria and tack one of the posters up. Having this bulletin board installed was one of the first things I did when I was elected community outreach officer. I'm pumped to see kids are using it to promote their JV games and band concerts, find study groups and tutors, and learn more about what's going on around our school and our town.

"Gotta Have Hope," Milo, our student council vice president, shouts in greeting, repeating my old campaign slogan.

"How goes it?" he asks with that JFK Middle–famous Milo smile.

"I'm doing great." I smile at him.

"I see you're making the most of your community outreach board," he says, giving me one of his elaborate fist bumps. "Nice!"

"Yup, and I'll personally give you one of these flyers because I know that means this info is as good as broadcasted."

"Funny you mention broadcasting this flyer," Milo starts. "I'm filming JFK Middle's first school

news show this afternoon. The school used to have one, but they pulled the plug on it years ago. But now we've brought it back!"

"That sounds awesome."

"It is." Milo nods, looking at the flyer. "And this is something cool I can report to the school. JFK Middle's science club is growing a garden and selling their veggies at the farmers' market? Nice!"

This is a great opportunity to get some publicity for the science club, so I tell Milo a little more about our plans. "It's our way of being eco-friendly and also raising money. We plan on donating some of what we grow to local food banks, too."

He must like what he hears, because Milo takes out his phone and asks me to repeat what I've said so he can voice-record it. Satisfied with this new info, Milo points at me as he starts inching away in preparation of continuing his social butterfly rounds. "Cool, thanks! Don't forget to check out the segment tomorrow morning."

"I won't."

I can't wait for everyone to learn more about what we're doing to help the planet.

☺🦋🌱

Before our first class the next day, my friends and I are gathered in the makers' space, our favorite lounge area at school. Word has gotten around that we can watch Milo's morning news show on the TV mounted there, so the room is packed with sixth graders and even some older kids.

"Maybe we can get Milo to air a few clips from our musical," Sam says to her fellow thespian Lacy.

"You know, that's a great idea," answers Lacy. "It could boost the musical's YouTube views way up."

Even though we're all having several mini conversations with one another, everyone quiets down when the show starts.

"Good morning, Tigers, and welcome to our first morning news program."

No surprise, Milo looks like he was born to be on TV. And somehow his charm and bright smile are even more mesmerizing on the screen.

"There's so much awesomeness happening at our school, and this is our way of highlighting the members of our community and the things they're doing that make us proud. This morning, we'd like to send a shout-out to the science club for starting a school garden, which—according to club member and community outreach officer Hope Roberts—will not only sell produce at the farmers' market in a few weeks but also donate some of what it grows to a local food bank. That's the Tiger spirit!"

We all whoop and holler at the screen, especially at the mention of the club and then again when my name rings out.

"Nice work!" Chloe shouts, giving me, Camila, and Grace high fives.

Grace and Camila beam at me, and I can't stop smiling. It feels great being recognized for our work in this way.

"Next up, we have some news everyone will be

eager to hear about," Milo continues. "NASA's latest rocket launch is this weekend, and school administrators have finally confirmed the viewing location for all eighth graders and a few lucky sixth and seventh graders."

Milo knows to pause for effect, because like a reflex, a loud cheer bursts out of us all.

"The location for the rocket launch viewing will be Woolly Pier." Gasps, each one bigger than the

next, escape from each of us. "Sixth and seventh graders will be given fifty slots per grade. Students can sign up online beginning tomorrow at seven a.m. The slots are first come, first served, so be sure to log on ASAP for your chance as this amazing opportunity!"

Everyone jots down the sign-in website address in their phones, on their hands, wherever—and with whatever—they have on them.

Milo continues in an enthusiastic tone. "The rest of the sixth and seventh graders are invited to watch the rocket launch in the school courtyard, where they can still get a distant glimpse of the rocket. Or you can always check out a broadcast of the launch online or on your TV at home."

"Ugh, that doesn't sound nearly as amazing as going to Woolly Pier," says Camila, biting her lower lip. "We've got to make sure we get onto that site and sign up."

We all nod in agreement, too lost in thought to say a word.

"Thank you for tuning in," says Milo, rocking his original camera angle. "This has been your morning news report. Have a great day, Tigers!"

The clang of the morning bell scatters the makers' space crowd, and our footwear stomps, squeaks, and click-clacks though the halls as everyone heads to class.

Chloe sidles up beside me and gives me a hello shoulder bump. "Garden tour in a few weeks? I want to see what everyone's raving about," she says with a wink.

I grin at the idea of our garden becoming one of

the cool spots to visit on campus. "You got it."

"Good luck with the rocket launch sign-ups," says Chloe. "Unless you don't need the luck because your dad already got you tickets?"

I give Chloe a half smile and a shrug, pretending that I'm keeping my plans a mystery. I don't want to admit to her or myself that there is no plan, and I don't even know the answer to her question.

Chloe laughs at my nonresponse, and we give each other a high five before heading in opposite directions down our school's main hallway.

☺♻♀

I don't know if it's the high five, the cool on-air shout-out from Milo, or the support from my friends, but soon I'm able to put the launch out of my head and focus on the positive. Maybe Milo's announcement about the garden will get more people thinking about how to be more eco-friendly at school and at home. Just like the server at the restaurant who asked her boss to switch to biodegradable take-out containers, there might be more people helping their families, friends, and teachers make decisions that are way healthier for our environment.

I'm encouraged thinking about these changes. But by lunchtime, when I'm grabbing my glass container out of my backpack and standing in the serving line in the cafeteria, it doesn't seem like Milo's message has really stuck. The only thing people seem to have remembered from the news show is to sign up for one of the open Woolly Pier rocket launch viewing slots tomorrow morning.

"I don't usually see you grabbing lunch this late," Henry says. He had slipped into the line behind me without me noticing.

"Hey!" I smile at him and pivot so that we're standing shoulder to shoulder. "I ran outside to check on the garden first."

"Cool." He glances at me from the corner of his eye. "I'm surprised you weren't stuck talking about the launch sign-ups. That's all anyone's talking about today."

Our line inches up, but only just a bit. There must be a delay—not that I mind. The extra time with Henry isn't so bad.

"Oh, wait, do you even need to sign up?" he asks. "Because of your dad working at NASA?"

I look down at my sneakers, feeling embarrassed for the second time today that I don't know the answer to that. I can't believe the launch is in just a few days and Dad hasn't said *anything* about family tickets.

"I don't think it works that way with an event this huge," I finally say. "But you're right—most kids aren't really thinking about the environment right now."

"Well, I gotta say, Camp Go Green inspired me to finally get my parents to start using the compost bin they got years ago."

"Congrats on getting them to take that next step!"

"Thanks, but it was only because I've been thinking so much about you—" Henry shakes his head, and the tips of his ears go bright red. "I mean, about the Go Green project you're doing at home and how you got Ms. Gordon to help with the garden and stuff."

Henry is wiping the damp off his forehead now, and I look away and try to hide my smile. I sorta feel better I'm not the only one who gets embarrassed when we talk. Good thing the line gets moving again and I'm getting a serving of spring rolls.

"I'll, uh, see you later." I wave to Henry and move on. I'm nearly to my table when I groan. *Ugh, I forgot to refill my water bottle.* When I head back toward the line, Henry is standing with a girl and a boy I don't recognize.

"Dude, Milo's show was cool," says the boy.

"I hope it's a regular thing," says the girl. Then she turns to Henry. "And the garden your science club is doing sounds like the right, eco-friendly thing to do. I love that!"

The other boy nods and rolls his eyes. "That girl Hope they mentioned, isn't she the same Hope who had like a million campaign posters all over school during the election? How is *that* caring for the environment?"

I stop in my tracks, and they all get busted looks on their faces when they realize I've heard them talking about me.

I look at Henry, and he opens his mouth in an attempt to explain, apologize, or something—I don't stick around to find out. I just smile and pretend that everything is rosy. And then I walk straight out of the cafeteria to go eat my lunch alone in a library study room.

Chapter 13

A loud buzzer snaps me out of a daydream just as I'm about to relive that cafeteria gossip moment from school this afternoon. I'm usually the first to complain that the buzzer on our dryer is obnoxious, but this time I'm grateful that I've been spared from going over that embarrassing scene yet again.

I'm home alone, so it's clear someone has programmed the dryer to go off at this time. I guess someone in my family forgot to cancel it. They know that part of the latest phase of our Go Green plan is to reduce our usual weekly dryer use a bit.

When I check what's in the dryer, I'm annoyed to

find Marie's clothes in there. I sigh. *She was sup-posed to use the clothesline for these things.*

My family has been getting better with some eco-friendly habits, but they clearly need more time to get used to the new clothesline. It's better when I just wash the clothes overflowing in the laundry hamper myself so I can avoid getting bummed later when I discover someone else has overused the dryer again.

In the time it takes for me to add a load to the washer, Marie comes home.

"Hey," she says, sticking her head into the laundry room.

"Hey," I answer. "I found your clothes in the dryer."

Marie is already heading to her room. "I'll get them later," she singsongs.

I roll my eyes, but I don't say anything else. *It's just one mistake*, I tell myself. *She'll do better next time.*

"Oops!" While I was coaching myself into chill mode, I poured a bit too much detergent into the washer. Oh well. Hopefully it won't make a difference.

Moving on with my afternoon checklist, I fully load the dishwasher, take down my clothes from the clothesline out back, and sort out the trash and recyclables.

By the time I'm finished with that, I get a text from Grace.

Can you check out the spreadsheets I just emailed you? If you think everything looks good, I'll send them to the rest of the science club.

Will do, I reply.

Grace's amazing spreadsheets deserve a bigger screen, so I leave the garage to grab my laptop from my room. Marie's in the shower now. I grin when I

hear her off-key singing. Poor Cosmo has the same pained look he usually has on his face whenever Marie sings. I scratch behind his ears and shut the door to my room to drown her out.

I settle onto a fuzzy pillow on my bed and scroll through Grace's files. One file is for the garden, and the other is for the air-quality tests.

The gardening spreadsheet is just as cool as I expect it to be. Grace has charted all the plants and their growth so far. There are pictures of the leafy sprouts in different stages of their progression. There's also a watering schedule, showing whose duty it is to check in on the garden on what days. Even though we've all been pitching in and sending Grace updates about what we're seeing, none of us could've ever put all that information together this nicely.

The gardening report looks super cute! Checking out the other file now, I text her.

Grace does it again. Another cool spreadsheet. That never stops sounding weird—who would have thought I'd ever use the words "cool" and "cute" to describe digital charts and bar graphs?

I study the results of the air-pollution test readings. The test kits Grace and Shep put together look like something you'd find inside an old remote control. There's a small motherboard with wires that have been programmed to detect certain pollutants in the air. It's pretty neat!

Of course, Grace has detailed where and when each reading was taken. The test was conducted during morning drop-off, afternoon pickup, and a control time at midday. We also performed readings at different locations—close to the car and bus pickup and drop-off sites and at the school entrances. We even took a reading inside the main hallway. We've collected so much data, and it's exciting.

This is good to go! I text Grace.

With my mind off Grace's creations, I become aware of Marie's singing—again.

"Is she still in the shower?" I ask Cosmo.

He looks back into my eyes but doesn't answer.

It's confirmed when I walk into the hall and see the bathroom door shut. *How long has she been in there?*

I knock on the door.

"That's a long shower, Marie!"

"Okay, okay," she whines. I'm surprised she isn't putting up a fight. She really must be in a good mood. Before I even turn my back, she strolls out of the bathroom, a cloud of lavender-scented soap trailing her. "Everyone's meeting at the coffee shop in like five minutes anyway."

"Was that supposed to be you being in a rush?" I'm honestly confused.

I shake my head and head to the kitchen for a quick snack before the laundry's done.

"See ya!" Marie shouts to me as she leaves. After an impossibly long shower, she's already dressed and ready to go. I give her a weak wave, finding it hard to hide how upsetting her water waste is to me. Still, I don't say anything and she leaves humming another tune.

There's one last thing to do before I can start my homework, and that's grab the clothes from the

washer. There can't be long left in the cycle. I go toward the laundry room and the first step I take inside is a slippery one. My foot slips on the sudsy foaminess pooling on the floor, and I totally wipe out.

I shout in surprise. What a disaster!

When I poured extra detergent into the load by mistake, I had no idea things would bubble up this bad! On my hands and knees, I crawl over to the washer to turn it off. It takes a few more slips to get there, but I do.

Once the washer is finally off, I sit there in the sudsy puddle and wonder how I got in so over my head with all these Go Green duties. It's all harder— and messier—than I thought it would be.

There's no one home to help me clean up. My parents are working late, and Marie just stepped out. I'll have to do this on my own. (What else is new?)

After sitting there in shock for a few minutes, I finally crawl over to the hamper, pull out a few towels, and start soaking up this mess. It's a good thing the floor in here is tiled. There's no damage to the house.

The only injury is to my feelings—just like when I overheard those kids at school today. I'm doing my best to help make the planet a better place, but I just can't seem to catch a break. I wonder how long that hurt will take to heal.

Chapter 14

Bright and early the next morning, I'm sitting groggy-eyed at my desk. My laptop is open and my hand is hovering over my keyboard, ready to click the link when the clock strikes seven. Like a hawk, I'm watching the seconds count down. You'd think I'm the one at the rocket launch station.

3 . . . 2 . . .

"Whoa! Down, girl!"

Rocket leaps her ginormous shaggy body right into my lap, fumbling my whole setup. After I shoo her down, I check my screen and groan. Rocket somehow entirely closed out of the web page. I seriously want to yelp like a wounded pup, but one look at Rocket's squishy face and I can't stay mad at her.

Recovering the page pretty quickly, I head back to grab a slot. It's barely a minute past 7:00 a.m., so I hardly lost any time at all. The link to register is glowing and I happily click it.

All slots have been filled.

What? Fifty sixth graders have claimed a slot in the first minute? It can't be. I wonder who those fifty people are. I'm disappointed for myself, but fingers crossed, at least my friends will turn out to be among the lucky—and super-quick—fifty.

Especially Camila. I can't imagine how bummed she'll feel if she doesn't score a spot to watch the launch.

My answer comes soon enough. Camila is already in her seat in science class when I arrive. It only takes a quick glance at her face to know that she didn't get one of the slots either.

"You too?" I ask as I slink into my desk.

Camila nods, her long lashes hooding the sadness in her eyes. "Of all things, my computer crashed at the worst time possible—6:59 a.m."

Ugh. I can almost physically feel her pain.

"I was up and running again a few minutes later, but even though it was only 7:02, I couldn't get a slot. The entire morning, I couldn't help thinking over and over: *If only I had been one minute earlier.*"

"Well, let me set your mind at ease with that last part. One minute earlier wouldn't have helped you," I say. "I logged in at 7:01 and the slots were already filled."

"No way!"

I give her the slow nod. "Yup."

She grimaces. "Yikes, I'm sorry."

"Camila, I'm the one who's sorry," I say, twisting to face her. "A few things happened yesterday that have made me realize how wrapped up I've been in my own Go Green mission. And because of that, I've missed out on valuable rocket launch geek-out moments with you."

"I admit, you *have* missed endless sessions with the space-travel fandom," she says. "But jokes aside, being at Camp Go Green really changed me, too. It changed a lot of us. We believe even more in the importance of caring for the earth. But you showed

us all how to *do something* with what we learned.
We were all inspired, but the difference is, you took
action."

"Thank you—that means a lot to hear you say
that," I say softly. In my next breath, I sit up tall
and speak loud and clear. "I believe in the importance of caring for my friends, too, so you name the
time and place, and I'll be ready to join the space-
travel fandom with you."

"Lunchtime at our usual table, of course," she
answers.

At that moment, Connor swaggers into the

classroom acting more boastful than usual. He stops short at Shep's desk, and the two of them bump elbows.

"See you at Woolly Pier!" Connor whoops.

That's two lucky people. Forty-eight more smiling sixth graders must be floating around somewhere.

When we meet up with Grace after class, she flashes us a smile and a thumbs-up sign. It makes total sense that Grace, the most organized person I know, got a slot the second the site was available. She's all about foolproof planning. Camila and I return a happy thumbs-up back at Grace. By the time we're on our way to lunch, we've counted at least six people who've made it onto the list. When I finally notice Sam's texts, that number rises up to nine people, because she, Lacy, and Golda are in!

We know we're going to hear about other lucky kids once we step foot in the cafeteria. But when I walk in, I feel eyes on me—even though I don't actually *see* anyone looking right at me. Maybe people are avoiding eye contact on purpose because they overheard what that boy said about me to Henry yesterday? Or maybe it's just my imagination.

Still, I wish I had walked in with Camila and Grace, but I had to offload a few books into my locker on the way. Today, I packed my lunch, so at least there's no need for me to stand in the serving line. Just a few more paces and I'll be with my friends.

I spot Camila and Grace at our usual table with a surprise guest—Chloe! Chloe looks up and waves wildly to me. I giggle and wave back, a goofy grin stretching my face. Just then, a different hand goes up and returns my wave. It's Henry. I see his sheepish smile first, before he pops up from his table and walks over to me.

"Hope, I'm so glad you're okay after what happened yesterday," he says. His ears are red-tipped again, and he sounds sincere. "That guy doesn't know how much you've been doing to help the planet."

"Thanks, Henry," I tell him, glancing up from my shoes. "I guess I *have* kind of gone on a Go Green deep dive lately. There's so much going on right now at home, and the garden and everything have been a nice distraction."

Henry smiles. "Well, you were cool enough to take us all with you on that deep dive. Thanks for that."

He holds out his fist, and I bump it with mine.

"What was that all about?" Chloe asks when I

join them at the table. She comes over to sit with us from time to time when she feels more like socializing than journaling. I'm glad she's sitting with us today.

"Nope." Camila holds out her hands to stop us from saying another word. "This lunch break is dedicated to everything space travel. So, Hope, what's the inside scoop?"

"I'm happy to swap theories, but I don't have any more behind-the-scenes knowledge than you do," I say softly. "Dad's been in his work cave these past few weeks."

"All this time, I imagined you were hoarding all the fascinating details for yourself," says Camila,

her eyes flashing regret. "I didn't realize." She reaches across the table and gives my hand a comforting squeeze.

"It's okay," I say honestly, and I squeeze her hand right back.

"Either way, Chloe and I will be sure not to hoard any details we catch at our Woolly Pier viewing," says Grace.

"We'll share videos, pics, everything," adds Chloe.

"Aw, thanks for taking one for the team," I say with oodles of sarcasm.

"Yeah, you guys are real heroes," Camila plays along. Then, as if Grace and Chloe aren't there, she says directly to me, "Hope, I've never wanted to have a food fight more than I do right this moment."

"Same," I say, menacingly holding a pinch of shredded cabbage.

"Hey, didn't anything Ms. Gordon said sink in?" Chloe giggles and ducks. "What happened to not wasting stuff?"

I slowly raise the cabbage from my plate higher and higher. Grace and Chloe look at me pleadingly and duck even lower. And then suddenly . . . I pop the cabbage in my mouth and eat it. We all crack up, and I can't help but think this is the most fun I've had in weeks.

Chapter 15

"That's a good girl!" I grin at Rocket and take the stuffed animal out of her mouth. She's getting so much better at sharing. I throw the fuzzy to the other side of the kitchen, where Cosmo is waiting patiently for it.

Buzz.

"What could that be?" I huff out in my dog-playing voice. I laugh at the puppy expressions looking back at me. And then something else occurs to me—is someone using the dryer instead of the clothesline? *Again?*

My pups are at my heels when I take a peek at the clothes inside the dryer. They look like my sister's, and there's barely anything in the load. That's the second day in a row. Why would she do this? I step out to the backyard to double-check the clothesline. The only things swaying in the wind are the dish towels I hung on the line this morning.

I march back into the house and follow the off-key humming to Marie's room.

"Marie, your clothes are ready," I say with an attitude.

"Okay." My sister's voice is muffled because she's facing her closet, talking into it instead of turning to face me. "I'll grab them in a bit—unless you want to get them for me?"

"Why should I do anything for you, when you can't even follow simple requests?" I say to the back of Marie's head. She hasn't even turned around to talk to me. I fold my arms, wondering why, just like with my Go Green lists, even this is too much to ask.

"You know the whole 'use the clothesline' idea isn't going to work for everything, don't you?" says Marie, with a casual, jokey tone to her voice. "It's a stretch to expect the rest of us to do this all the

time. Besides, I thought you volunteered to pick up the slack for some of those tasks."

I let out a dramatic sigh. "Yeah, for now. But my hope was that you guys would join in and help when you can."

Somehow, my sister is deeper into her closet now. It makes me wonder if maybe she's got some magical portal like Galaxy Girl that takes her to her coffeehouse meetups. "Isn't that the point of us trying out eco-friendly changes?" her muffled voice asks. "So we can see which changes work for us?"

I feel my whole face crinkle up in confusion. "How does not running a near-empty dishwasher or dryer not work for you?"

Marie finally emerges from her closet, each hand clutching a few garments. "So, this is your idea of talking to reach a solution? All you're doing is accusing me of not doing enough."

I raise my eyebrows. "Well, you're kind of not." There, I said it. I don't mean to insult Marie, but I

don't want to lie to her, either. Today's empty dryer was the last straw.

She throws the fistfuls of garments onto an already-tall pile of clothes on her bed.

"You know what, Hope? *You're* the one not doing enough."

"Me?" I almost shriek.

"Yes, you—*you're* not paying enough attention. I don't know if you've noticed, but everyone is always crunched for time these days. Yet we are trying to

be good sports and hear you out. Yes, I may still forget to use my thermos every now and then, and I'm tired of having my trash audited. But if you don't see how we're trying to help even at a busy time, then maybe you just don't want to see it."

Marie picks up her clutch purse and her phone, and she storms past me, down the hall, and out the front door.

What just happened?

I'm super confused. My brain wants to solve for x, and my stomach just feels like it's in knots. It's not a great feeling knowing your sister is fed up with what she considers to be pushy demands. I never wanted to turn anyone away from what I'm trying to do.

And I never imagined working hard for the planet could lose me a few points with people who used to support me.

I drag my feet back to my room, and my dogs automatically seem to think that I'm about to give them a treat.

"Greedy goobers," I tease them with a sad smile before giving them each a doggy biscuit. When they settle on my plush rug for a nap, I hop in my bed and cozy up with my laptop. I go straight to Camp Go Green's website and look at the gorgeous pictures showing the leafy landscape I visited a few weeks ago. It was challenging working in the camp garden and creepy to step into the forest at night. But the whole experience meant so much to me. Never did I imagine my new eco-friendly goals for my family would be so hard to live by.

Everyone has a million and one things they'd rather be thinking about or doing than focusing on the environment. Nothing I can do will keep their attention away from all of that. *And if I try, I come off looking like I'm too demanding*, I think to myself.

Absentmindedly, I click on a video on the home page. The thumbnail shows Ms. Gordon in the woods. "Everyone should have a 'sit spot'—a place outdoors where they can sit quietly, observe, reflect, and be with nature," explains Ms. Gordon in the video. "Find your sit spot today and spend a little time there."

That's exactly what I decide to do. I power off my laptop and go to the backyard. My dogs pop up from their slumber and follow me.

A cool patch of grass in the shade looks like it would make the perfect sit spot. Just like Ms.

Gordon suggested, I plop myself down and sit quietly. Eventually Cosmo and Rocket stop circling, lie out, and chill. That's when I really start paying attention . . . to the birds, the swaying palms, the scent of the ocean across town.

After a few peaceful minutes, other things begin to come to my attention. My mind plays back some of the conversations I've had with my friends this week. Chloe, Henry, and Camila have all asked about Dad. A sadness hits me and bubbles up my throat.

Dad and the rocket launch.

This is something I've been counting down to, just like Camila. Only Camila doesn't hide her enthusiasm or distract herself from it. But my own excitement is mixed with frustration over my dad shutting me out. I know he's not doing this on purpose, but I can't help but feel that way.

As the thoughts pop up, I stay still and silent. I just sit there and observe everything. Thinking about Dad leads to me thinking about my argument with Marie and my pushy behavior with my family over the past few weeks.

I thought by focusing on going green, I could show my family that these habits aren't so hard to pick up. But, in the end, I have to admit that it's not as easy to go green as I thought. It's definitely a lifestyle change, and some days are more challenging than others. If I can't do this, how do I expect my family to?

It's only when my legs fall asleep that I realize I need to jump back into action.

When I step inside, I'm alone with Cosmo and Rocket. Marie still isn't home. The wayward shoebox in front of the door leading to our garage makes me look in there.

Whoa.

There are more old shoeboxes and shipping boxes

lining the far wall of the garage with what looks like bags of clothes for donation. Did Marie really empty out her closet? This sure looks like her handiwork—especially since the boxes aren't in the right place for recycling pickup. My heart filled with gratitude, I get to work on the boxes, breaking them down and stuffing them in the recycling bins. It feels good to help Marie after she worked so hard to clear out her closet. I'm only hoping she forgives me for assuming she hadn't been trying to change old habits.

When they get home not too long later, my parents find me rummaging in the recycling bins. The sunlight from the now-open garage door fills the

space with glowy sunshine. I'm close to done flattening all of Marie's boxes and prepping for recycling pickup. The bin is stashed and towering.

"Uh-oh," says my dad as he approaches my corner of the garage. He and my mom walk into the garage instead of parking inside. "Have I been working this hard? How did I not notice that our garage has turned into a recycling center?"

I wipe my forearm against my sweaty brow. When I look at my dad with a weak smile, concern lines instantly appear on Mom's face.

"Hope?" she asks softly. "Something wrong?"

"Nothing . . . anymore," I say, taking a slow breath. "This is going to sound corny, but the calming power of nature helped me realize a few things about myself. I see now that I've been rushing people to action. I just hope that I haven't turned everyone off to helping the planet."

"Never that," answers Mom. "The way I see it, each earthling has a role in reversing the damage we're doing to the planet. Some start bigger than others, but that doesn't mean smaller contributions don't still matter."

Dad reaches a hand to my shoulder and shakes

his head thoughtfully. "I'm sorry we haven't caught up in a while—especially about the rocket launch. I know how much it means to you."

Without warning, my eyes cloud over with heavy tears that threaten to shower down. But oddly, I feel relieved when a light stream travels down my cheeks. Dad embraces me.

"I'm sorry," he says gently.

"I guess I kinda threw myself into saving the planet to distract myself from thinking about you and how I was missing out on details about the rocket launch," I admit, pulling away from Dad to take a tissue from Mom and clean myself up. "But environmental science actually became so fascinating to me. It really is super interesting."

"I'm glad you learned more about it, because it has benefited all of us," Mom chimes in.

"And hey, I haven't mentioned it yet," Dad says, "but, kiddo, I appreciate the changes you've made to our household habits." He playfully joins his palms in prayer. "Especially the fact that you mercifully started with small changes."

Mom pretends to close her eyes and pray, and I can't help but give a little chuckle. I dry my tears and smile at my parents.

"With time," Dad continues, "I'm sure we will all be ready for some bigger ones." He whispers out of the side of his mouth, "Extra emphasis on the word *some*."

The laughter I break out with now seems to ease more of the tension I've been feeling this week.

"Pretty soon, the Roberts household will be onto green engineering like at NASA," Dad says proudly.

"What do you mean by 'green engineering'?" I ask, extra curious.

"Well, there are a lot of exciting developments to balance out the pollution involved in space travel," he tells Mom and me. Dad explains that there are more eco-friendly materials being used in this launch, along with engineering advancements that focus on emission-free solutions. "In fact, the astronauts will be performing environmental studies on this rocket-launch mission."

A lightbulb goes off in my mind, an idea that I think would make an awesome surprise for science club. But before I can say anything, my mom speaks up with her own bright idea.

"Going green, the rocket launch, all this recyclable waste!" she shouts, claps, and hops excitedly.

Dad and I give each other a look because we can't decipher what her word clues could mean.

"Don't you see? I've finally got it!" She stops bouncing and holds out her hands to brace us for her big idea. "For the town's public arts project, we'll commission artists to create artwork from reclaimed pieces in celebration of the rocket launch!"

"Ohmygosh, that's fantastic!" Dad shouts, giving my mom a hug.

"I love it!" I say, throwing my arms around the both of them.

It's super exciting to know this artwork will be space-travel themed and will be displayed through-out the city! Marie returns home right as the rest of the family is celebrating Mom's brilliance.

Despite obviously wanting to stay mad at me, Marie grins when I yank her into our family group hug. I know my family has my back, so I decide to take Marie's advice and be more patient.

Besides, small changes add up.

Chapter 16

'**ve** got something extra special planned for
Friday's science club, and it's not just our presentation to Ms. Reimer. Weirdly, I'm not as nervous
about presenting our air-quality report as I am
about this special surprise. I just hope everything
goes well.

When Ms. Reimer walks into the science lab to
hear from us, we convince her to go on a quick tour
of the garden first. She's impressed to see how far
it's come in just a few weeks, and she promises to
buy some cucumbers from our first farmers' market
booth.

When we get back inside a few minutes later, all

our members are ready to talk about the different areas of our pollution test—the observations, the coding, and the meter readings. Ms. Reimer listens thoughtfully, only interrupting to ask questions about information she'd like clarified.

When it's Camila's and my turn to share our recommendation for next steps, my dad walks in and quietly takes a seat in the back of the room. Camila shoots me a quizzical look, but she and I continue with the presentation.

"As the meter readings team reported, our air-quality findings show that a significant reading was detected fifty feet from the bus parking circle," I say, switching my focus back to Ms. Reimer. "Our recommendation is that the buses drop off fifteen to twenty feet back from where they do now. It'll be a little more distance for riders to walk, but they'll be breathing clearer air while they do it."

Ms. Reimer scribbles on the tiny spiral notebook she carried in.

Camila points to the school map posted on the whiteboard behind us. "Our recommendation with the carpool lane is for drivers to cut off their car engines instead of idling. This will reduce the circulating fumes significantly."

More scribbling from Ms. Reimer. I can't tell whether this is a good sign or not.

At the conclusion of our presentation, Ms. Reimer, Mr. G., and Dad applaud.

"You've given me a lot to discuss with our principal and school board members, but my hunch is they will offer their support to allow us to make these helpful adjustments." Ms. Reimer thanks us, and once she leaves the room, everything is silent and still.

As soon as we hear her footsteps recede down the hall, it's our turn to cheer. Even Connor seems pumped about it. We all fist-bump, high-five, and hug one another, until Mr. G. calms us all down.

"We are in for a big treat today before we conclude

our meeting. Thanks to one of our members calling in a few favors with a close relative, we have a special guest here from NASA to speak to us about what to expect at the upcoming rocket launch."

Gasps echo throughout the room, and Camila squeezes my hand so tightly, I wince.

"I'm sorry!" she sputters. "It's just that this is the best surprise!"

"Take a seat, everyone, and get ready for our guest speaker," says Mr. Gillespie.

I feel so proud seeing my dad walk to the front of the room and smile at everyone. He looks a bit tired, but he looks so happy. When he gives me a little wave, I throw up my hand and wave back.

"I wasn't sure if I could pull off this visit, so I asked my daughter not to share it with anyone other than Mr. Gillespie. But I'm glad I got the chance to come speak to you about some of the green engineering advances scientists are utilizing at this weekend's rocket launch. We'll also talk about some of the work our team will be doing toward better understanding the impact of pollution and how we can reverse the damage."

As my dad talks, he takes questions from curious science club members who just can't wait until the end of his presentation. They remind me of all my burning questions lobbed at Ms. Gordon.

"Is a rocket launch bad for the environment?" Camila asks.

"I'm glad you asked that, even though the answer isn't a simple one." We listen closely as Dad talks about the different types of rockets used in launches, and how they each use different types of fuels—some less toxic than others.

"But what about that huge cloud of smoke we see at the base of the rocket when it takes off?" asks Henry.

"Well, that's actually just steam," he says, raising his finger as Ms. Gordon would.

"Whoa," says Connor and a few other people echo him.

Whoa is an understatement. My mind is blown from Dad's talk, and I'm so happy he came. After the last question is answered, Camila almost stands up and cheers.

Dad holds up his hands to quiet the applause. "I almost forgot—there's one final thing even my daughter knows nothing about." Dad looks at me and winks. "I secured a few slots at NASA's VIP oceanside viewing location for the science club. I've sent the info to Ollie—I mean, Mr. Gillespie—and I can't wait to see you all there."

Everyone whoops and hollers like they've been invited to suit up and travel through the stratosphere. "Woo-hoo!"

My dad might as well be a rock star for all the screaming breaking out around him. We'd lift him over our heads if we all could. Instead, I settle for giving Dad a huge hug.

There's no doubt today is a victory for Mr. Gillespie and his science gang, but it's also an encouraging moment for me.

☺🐾🌱

The first thing I do when I get home is open my laptop. I want to share the latest updates about the garden and our air-quality test with Ms. Gordon in an email. But when I log on, there's an email in my inbox from someone I don't recognize.

"Who could this be?" I ask Cosmo, who is sitting on my lap.

Before I draft my email to Ms. Gordon, I open it.

Hello, and greetings from the great state of Georgia. I am emailing to report where I found your message plank. I plucked it out of Lake Buligari in Swank County. My dog took a liking to your plank, and so it now serves as her chew toy. I've attached a photo of my pup playing with it. All my best to you in your corner of the world. Best, Scarlett Miller

Cosmo barks at the puppy in the photo and attempts to sniff my laptop screen.

I immediately look up the location of the lake. "Amazing! Do you see that, Cosmo?" I ask my unaware pooch. "It's over two hundred miles away, which means it flowed up the river and past a few tributaries until it joined with the lake."

I reread the email and shake my head in awe. We are all connected. That's why I know that if we all work together, we truly can save the planet.

Chapter 17

The skies are blue, bright, and clear on the day of the launch. Mom, Marie, and the whole science club are here, along with Mr. Gillespie and one special guest.

"Thanks for inviting me, Hope," says Ms. Gordon. "This is neat!"

"Well, you showed us the nature-made wonders of a night hike, so we thought we'd dazzle you with something human-made."

Camila clambers over with her selfie stick extended out to its limit. "Everyone, let's take a quick group selfie before the launch," she says. "Ms. Gordon, get in here!"

We all laugh as Camila snaps a few times.

"This is the coolest thing in the world," Camila repeats again. "Please tell your dad we said thank you for this."

"You can tell him yourself if you come with us to the town center in a couple of weeks. The mayor is having a different kind of launch party for the unveiling of Mom's citywide art installation."

A group of select artists are working on creating rockets using repurposed waste, and they will be

installed all over town—at the beach promenade, outside the library, in the town center itself, and in more eye-catching places. We are so proud we'll get to celebrate this moment with Mom.

"I'm there," says Grace. "It's such a cool theme. The whole town is excited about it."

"I'm hoping the people are as excited about the environmental-science theme as they are the rocket-science one," I say.

Ms. Gordon overhears us and walks over. "I think people are starting to get it," she says, with a slight smile. "We need to clean house, because the earth is our home."

I think about Ms. Gordon's words as we witness two citizens of the earth catapult out of the stratosphere. The rumbling energy of both the rocket and our emotions shakes us all to the core. Camila wipes a tear from her cheek, and I hold her hand. Grace takes my other hand and we watch, feeling as connected as

ever. Henry glances at me, and we smile warmly at each other before fixing our gazes to the sky.

Suddenly, I'm filled with hope about all the work humans are doing both in the stratosphere and on the ground to save the planet.

The feeling makes me so happy, I feel like I'm floating in zero gravity.

But when look at my feet, they're firmly planted on Earth. And I know, I'm just getting started on my work here.

HOPE'S TIPS

There are so many ways to care for this planet we call home—and so many people dedicated to saving it. Brave Swedish activist Greta Thunberg tirelessly calls attention to the climate crisis. And Mari Copeny is an American champion for safe drinking water. These young activists inspire me to do all I can to make eco-friendly changes in my own community. Everything you do to help makes an impact. Leading by example isn't easy, but I keep it going, because the earth is worth it!

Here are some tips on how you can go green, too!

Reduce, reuse, recycle: Try adjusting your everyday habits to be eco-friendlier. When you buy new clothes, books, or games, try looking for gently used options first. Then be sure to donate the ones you no longer want. Don't forget to keep reusable bags, water bottles, and metal straws handy. And think about how you can reduce emissions to the atmosphere, too. Choose carpools or catch the bus; walk or ride your bike. Now you're totally on the road to having the earth's back!

Buy local: Getting fresh veggies from your backyard garden, a farmers' market, or a grocer that sources local farms are great ways to give back to Mother Nature. The shorter distance your food travels to get to your table, the less packaging waste and transportation emissions are added to the environment. Plus, it's a cool way to support farmers in your area!

Explore the outdoors: It doesn't take a special trip to somewhere like Camp Go Green to enjoy your environment. Plan a simple outing with your family or take a walk with your human or canine friends. Don't be a stranger to the outdoors. The more we bond with them, the more inclined we'll be to protect green spaces near and far.

Contact your elected officials: Most of the world's pollution is caused by corporations, not people like you and me. Thankfully, laws can be enacted to prevent businesses from hurting our environment. Let your officials hear from you, too! Call or email your state and federal representatives and demand that they address green issues like climate change.

Stay informed: Camp Go Green's website was a great resource for me. Find your own go-to source for all things green. The Environmental Protection Agency's website for students (epa.gov/students) is a great place to get started. As you learn more about climate change and what we can do to stop it, share this knowledge with your teachers and family. The planet is depending on us to stay on top of this crisis. Your help can mean all the difference in the world.

About the Author

Dirk Franke

ALYSSA MILANO began acting when she was only 10 years old. She has continued to work in both TV and movies since then, including hit shows like *Who's the Boss?* and *Charmed*. Alyssa is also a lifelong activist who is passionate about fighting for human rights around the world. She has been a National Ambassador for UNICEF since 2003, and she enjoys speaking to students in schools around the country about the importance of voting. She was named one of *Time* magazine's Persons of the Year in 2017 for her activism. Alyssa lives in Los Angeles with her husband and two kids. This is her first children's book series.

About the Author

Chanda Williams

DEBBIE RIGAUD is the coauthor of Alyssa Milano's Hope series and the author of *Truly Madly Royally*. She grew up in East Orange, New Jersey, and started her career writing for entertainment and teen magazines. She now lives with her husband and children in Columbus, Ohio. Find out more at debbierigaud.com.

About the Illustrator

ERIC S. KEYES is currently an animator and character designer on *The Simpsons*, having joined the show in its first season. He has worked on many other shows throughout the years, including *King of the Hill*, *The Critic*, and *Futurama*. He was also a designer and art director on Disney's *Recess*. Hope is his first time illustrating a children's series. Eric lives in Los Angeles with his wife and son.

Change the world with HOPE in these four stories!

FROM *NEW YORK TIMES* BESTSELLING CREATORS
ALYSSA MILANO, DEBBIE RIGAUD, AND ERIC S. KEYES!